GW00535553

Issue Two

Editors
Ginny Baily and Sally Flint

Front Cover Image
Ruth Oakley

Printed by **imprintdigital.net** Exeter

Published 2008 by Dirt Pie Press

The Editors would like to acknowledge the support of the Creative
Writing and Arts Department in the School of Arts, Languages and
Literature at the University of Exeter.

www.riptidejournal.co.uk

ISBN 978-0-9558326-0-4

Contents

Introduction

I've always loved short stories. Their structure; their variety; their uniqueness. The impact of a good short story can be much more immediate than that of a novel, and with fewer plot strands to assimilate and fewer characters to introduce, the details of a story can linger in memory long after those of a novel have been forgotten.

To some the short story is an underrated form, dismissed as insubstantial, inferior to the novel by reason of its brevity. I believe that quite the opposite is true. It takes a greater discipline, a different talent to write a good short story. The reader's attention must be gained within the first couple of paragraphs; the length and structure of the work must be perfectly balanced; momentum must be carefully calculated and it must resolve at the end like a piece of music, leaving the reader satisfied.

There is a different art to reading them, too - not too many at a time. Ideally, like poetry, each story requires some thinking time; time to reflect; to assimilate; to bid goodbye to one fictional universe before attempting to enter another. Sometimes this is a challenge; something of an intellectual effort. But a good story is worth the attempt. These little glimpses of other lives, other cultures are precisely what make reading worthwhile; and in a world in which time is always at a premium, the short story is ideal for the ones of us who have less time than we'd like to pursue our love of reading. Ten minutes on the Tube; in the bath; ten minutes before bedtime – that's all it takes to be hooked for life.

That's why it's my great pleasure to introduce this collection. Some of the authors are new, some will be familiar names. The stories themselves are by turns witty; subversive; thought-provoking; disturbing – but always well-written, and always sincere. I hope you'll enjoy them as much as I did. And I hope that you will revisit them, as I often do with short stories, whenever you need a change of perspective, a glimpse into another world, or just a quick fix of something new.

The next ten minutes could change your world. Indulge yourself – jump in!

Joanne Harris

The Death of the Aardvark

Robin Sidwell

It's been a few hours since the death of the Aardvark, though it feels like any other morning. Actually, I can't say for sure that it feels like any other morning, 'cause I'm never awake at three in the morning, but I imagine this is what it usually feels like. Strange, the way life's just carrying on. Lewis fidgets in the bed across from me, a toilet flushes, footsteps echo on the grated metal floor above and below us, the cleaners slam buckets down and gripe about what a shitty time of day it is to be cleaning. They should try living here. Anyway, point is that it could just be a regular morning on C Block. Only difference is, I know I'm not the only one awake.

A door slides shut, the sound clattering around the wing, reminding me how it used to wake me when I first got here and how now I sleep through it. Raymer whistles the music from the Typhoo advert as he completes his second circuit. Peterson yells at him to shut the fuck up. He says it in a Mexican accent. Raymer looks up, spinning around as if he might catch a glimpse of the sound before it disappears.

'I know who said that!' he yells back. 'I know who that was!'

'Yeah?' Peterson yells. 'Good. 'Cause your mother's a fucking flid!' Someone above us, probably Adam Rucks – or Rukus, as he's known in here – stifles a laugh. Everybody's awake. Ain't nobody gonna sleep tonight.

***

C Block's one of seven wings housing kids aged fifteen to nineteen, most of them petty criminals. It's not a bad block to be on - better than being cooped on B Block, with all the rapists and psychos. I was on B Block for my first week, while they waited for a space to open up. Trust me, the place is full of sickos. Even when you're queuing for dinner, some fucker's clocking your ass. These are people who were fucked up sexually *before* they came here. It gets real fucking cosy over there, believe me. Real fucking cosy. C Block's fucking CenterParcs, compared to B Block.

I've been on C Block almost a year. We've got some of the best wardens – discounting Raymer – and quite a few characters. One of those characters was the Aardvark. The Aardvark arrived here from G Block a week ago. The wardens told us he was here on drugs charges, but we all knew the truth. The Aardvark had done something a lot worse than heroin. He'd informed. They sent him here when he stopped co-operating.

Let me tell you something about being inside. Inside, informers are the lowest of the low and, after spending six months on G Block, the Aardvark's secret had gotten round. One of the new prisoners recognised him and a couple of days later, someone stabbed him with a fork. The upshot of it was that they moved him onto our wing. By the time they moved him though, word was out.

The Aardvark probably strikes you as a pretty strange name, but trust me, *everybody* in this place has a nickname. Mine's Long John. It came about 'cause when you arrive here, they issue you with a pair of long johns. Nobody wears them. It's like the thing with our badges. Nobody wears their badge on their t-shirt, like you're supposed to. You can wear your badge anywhere you like but don't wear it on your t-shirt, for Christ's sake. You'll never hear the end of it. It's funny, even though we all wear identical blue uniforms, people still manage to start these little trends. Anyway, on my first night here, I wore my long johns and that's where the name comes from. Nowadays people call me Johnny. My real name's Warren. The wardens call me 325.

***

I was in the dinner hall first time I saw the Aardvark. I was sitting with Lewis – my cell mate – and Whitey and Peterson. They were talking about the world cup. England were set to play Argentina and Lewis had bet Peterson ten cigarettes that Sven wouldn't play Heskey. Lewis must have had a serious gambling problem on the outside. The kid couldn't refuse a bet if his life depended on it. Anyway, the Aardvark came in with Waters and Raymer and they sat in the far corner, a couple of tables down from us.

'There he is,' Whitey said, pointing at them with his fork and making a quick, stabbing motion. 'The informer, from G Block.'

'He looks like a right pussy.' Lewis glanced over his shoulder. 'What's the plan?'

'We're working on it,' Peterson told us. 'Raymer and the others are gonna be watching him real close, so we've gotta take our time.'

Rukus came over and sat down with us. 'Who's the new kid?'

'That's the informer,' Whitey said. 'The one from G Block.'

'Yeah?' Rukus stood up and peered over at him, before catapulting a spoonful of Smash towards the back of his head. It missed and hit the wall. Stuff may as well be glue, I swear down. You could hang your fucking posters with it. Anyway, Raymer leapt up and came charging over. We all sat there, eating our dinner in silence as he stood at the end of the table, arms folded. It was Peterson who caved first, exploding a giggle through his nose.

'Who threw the food?' Raymer said.

'What food?'

'That food,' Raymer said, pointing to the dollop of Smash that was still stuck to the wall.

Nobody responded.

'Somebody threw it,' Raymer said. 'Somebody had to have thrown it for it to end up there.' Let me tell you something about Raymer. If there was a Nobel Prize for stating the obvious, Raymer would win the fucking thing.

'You lot just behave,' Raymer told us. 'Anyone throws anymore food, you're all going to forfeit the next England game. Understand?'

We all nodded. He turned and walked away.

'The informer's dead,' Lewis said, when Raymer had gone. 'People are gonna be queuing up to bash him.'

'Yeah, well they'll just have to wait,' Whitey told him, stuffing a slice of Spam into his mouth. 'The informer's mine. And I'm gonna fuck him up good.'

Let me tell you something about Kenny White. Kenny White runs C Block. He's in here for armed robbery – which is about as bad as it gets on this wing – and *nobody* fucks with him. Luckily for me we get on. We're not exactly bum chums, but I share with Lewis and Whitey respects Lewis, so he cuts me slack. Ask me, Peterson's the one you've gotta watch.

Peterson's his sidekick. He walks with a limp and he's got a home made tattoo of a spider web on his left hand, between his thumb and forefinger. Peterson gets a lot of respect in here, but it's got nothing to do with how hard he is. The reason people respect Peterson is because he makes us laugh and trust me, if you can make people laugh in here, they'll love you for it. Just 'cause he plays the clown though, it doesn't mean he's stupid. Ask me, Peterson's probably the smartest kid in here. It's Peterson that's behind ninety per cent of the trouble and nine times out of ten, somebody else takes the blame.

***

Now let's get one thing straight. I'm no friend of the informer and I never will be. Having said that, I had no intention of hurting the Aardvark. They're reviewing me in a couple of weeks, so the way I saw it, best thing I could do was keep my head down. Certainly it wasn't worth fucking everything up just for the sake of bashing some junky.

So as you can imagine, I was as surprised as anyone when I found myself talking to him one time, during association. He'd only been here a few days and I was walking through the recreation area when he caught my eye. He was on his own, sitting on the floor, with his back against the wall, reading. I knew that Whitey had told us all to stay away, but I couldn't help it, not once I'd spotted what he was reading. And it's not like I intended to hurt him. I only wanted to ask him about his comic.

'What's that you're reading?' I asked, approaching him.

'Just a comic,' he muttered. 'Just a bit of Manga.' He spoke like a typical smack head – all in monotone – even had one of those bum fluff moustaches they try to grow. 'Street Fighter Two,' he added, without looking up.

'Volume one?' I asked.

'Yeah.'

'Second issue?'

'Yeah,' he looked up, 'That's right.'

I snapped my fingers in the air. 'You and me have gotta talk!'

'Why? D'you like Manga?'

'Do I like Manga?' I knelt down beside him, I couldn't let an opportunity to talk about Manga comics just pass me by. 'Do *I* like Manga? Let me tell you something, I *love* Manga. 'Specially Street Fighter. I've got the whole series.'

'D'you collect them, then?'

'Do I collect them? Do I collect them? Sure I collect them! Do you?'

'Yeah,' he put his comic down, 'I got into them a couple of years ago. I've got loads of them. They're in my cell.' He caught my eye. 'I've even got the first edition of the X Files.'

'You're takin' the piss?'

'I swear down.' He put his hand across his chest – kid was a junky and an informer, so as far as I was concerned, he could've been swearing on his mother's grave and it would have meant jack shit to me, but as it was, I believed him. 'I got it on Ebay,' he added.

'Shit, man!' I shook my head. 'D'you know how rare that is?'

'Sure. I paid through the nose for it.' He laughed faintly. 'It's the only thing I haven't sold,' he said, 'over the years.' The bell went, signalling the end of association.

'Hey, lissen,' I said, 'I wanna ask you one favour.'

'Go on…'

'What's your name?'

'Lee.'

'Lee. I want you to borrow me your X Files comic. I know you don't know me but I won't rob it, I swear down. I just wanna have a borrow of it.'

'Hey Johnny!' Someone called my name. 'Johnny! Get over here!' It was Peterson and Rukus. I stood up.

'In a bit,' I muttered, falling into line with them.

'Long John,' Peterson said.

'Peterson. How's tricks?'

'Good.' Peterson put his arm around me. 'Listen, Johnny. What the fuck are you doin' talkin' to that piece of shit?'

'Nothing, man. He's just asked me the time, that's all. I was just tellin' him the time.' It was a blatant lie. None of us wear watches.

'That cocksucker's marked,' Peterson said.

'Yeah, I know …'

'And as soon as Raymer leaves him alone for five minutes, Whitey's gonna make his move.'

'Course.'

'He ain't got no friends in this place. If I were you, I wouldn't be seen talking to him again. Even if it is to tell him the time. You get me?'

'Yeah, I get you.'

'Good lad.' He slapped me across the shoulders and turned his attention back to Rukus.

***

Later that day we had cell inspection with Waters. As he entered, he dropped a copy of the first edition of the X Files onto my bed.

'From Lee,' he muttered and then, turning to Lewis, 'Mr Lewis. How are we today?'

Waters always calls us by our names. He always says 'we' as well - like 'shall *we* do this,' - as if he's got to do it too. He's a good bloke, is Waters, not that it does him any favours. Peterson specialises in making his life hell and everybody loves him for it.

After Waters had left, Lewis asked me about the comic.

'What's that then?'

'Nothin', just a comic.'

He stood up and came over. 'X F-i-u-l-e-s.' Let me tell you something about Lewis. The kid can't read for shit. 'Ain't that the one you're always on about?' he asked. 'The rare one.'

'Yep,' I rolled onto my side and opened the first page. I couldn't believe I was actually holding the first edition of the X Files.

'Who's Lee?' Lewis asked. 'I don't know any Lee.'

'Lee's the kid who borrowed it me.'

'Lee?'

'Just this kid.'

'Is he new?'

'Yeah.'

'That's the Aardvark, then.'

I put the comic down. 'Look, it's just a comic. I mean, I know what the kid done. I know he's a prick, but you know how much I've always wanted to get my hands on the first edition of the X Files. How many times have I done your head in rambling on about this comic?'

'S'pose' Lewis said. 'Hey, forget it. It's cool.' He lay down on his bed with his hands behind his head and closed his eyes. That was the last time we spoke about it.

***

Although Whitey had said he was biding his time, his patience obviously ran out because the next day he introduced himself to the Aardvark. It was Sunday and we had two-hour association. Tyler Jander – Jango – had forfeited his association after pissing through his bars onto the recreation area, so he was in his cell. Whitey was on the pool table, playing Lewis. Everybody else was either milling around the table or watching the t.v. Suddenly, Jango started yelling at the top of his voice that Raymer was a fat queer – except he wasn't really yelling it, so much as singing it, operatic style. Everybody went wild and Raymer took off up the stairs, with Waters close behind him. Now, you ask me, the whole thing was set up, 'cause straight away, Whitey put his cue down and turned to the Aardvark.

'Hey! Aardvark!' This was the first time the Aardvark had actually been called the Aardvark, so initially he didn't respond. Of course, everybody knew who Whitey was talking to. There are no real Aardvarks on C Block, so he obviously meant the new kid. Being the new kid, the Aardvark didn't understand. He just stood there, sipping his tea from a polystyrene cup, nervously watching Helen Daniels raking leaves in an old episode of Neighbours.

'Yo! Aardvark!' Whitey yelled at the top of his voice. This time the Aardvark did look up. Whitey nodded at him. The Aardvark looked around for a moment, before pointing at himself and mouthing, 'Me?'

'Yeah, you. Aardvark.' A few people sniggered. Whitey leaned an outstretched arm on the back of one of the chairs. 'What's with the badge?'

'This badge?' the Ardvark muttered, fingering the badge on his t-shirt.

'That's the one,' Whitey said.

'Just my number,' the Aardvark said.

'Oh right,' Whitey took a step forward. 'What? Your phone number?' Everybody started to laugh. The Aardvark started to laugh too, but you could tell he didn't get what was funny.

'It's my I.D,' he muttered. 'They gave it …'

'Where's mine?' Whitey yelled, grabbing the front of his t-shirt and pretending to desperately search for his badge. Everyone was laughing now. We all know that Whitey wears his badge on his sock. 'Hey, Peterson!' he said, turning to Peterson, 'have you got a badge on your t-shirt?'

'Nope,' Peterson said, making a show of checking his t-shirt. 'I usually wear my badge on my inside trouser leg.'

'Hey, Long John! You got a badge on yours?'

'No,' I said, 'I wear my badge on my trouser pocket.'

'Funny that,' Whitey said, "cause the Aardvark seems to have a badge on his t-shirt. *And* it's a different colour.'

'A different colour?' Peterson said.

'Yeah,' Whitey said. 'Take a look at it. It's blue.'

'Oh yeah.' Peterson scratched his head. 'I wonder why.'

'I think,' Whitey said slowly, as if he was just working this one out, 'That blue's the badge they give you on G Block.'

'I think you might be right,' Peterson said. 'You weren't on G Block, were you, Aardvark?'

'For a while,' the Aardvark said in a hoarse whisper, 'to begin with.'

'Interesting,' Whitey said, making a show of weighing this information. 'How come they moved you?' He took a step towards him. 'Beds not comfortable enough?' Everybody laughed. The Aardvark didn't answer. He'd begun to sweat, visibly. The place had taken on that atmosphere it always does when it's about to kick off. It would have gone off then and there, if Raymer hadn't suddenly come trotting down the stairs, his steel toe-capped boots clomping on the metal. The crowd dispersed. Whitey quickly turned back to the pool table and the game resumed. Rukus hit a button on the remote and the t.v. was back on. Raymer did a quick circuit of the room, looking deadly serious. Whitey sunk the black and Lewis handed over a phone card, muttering something about the Aardvark affecting his concentration. The Aardvark just stood there, pretending to be watching the t.v. He understood who Whitey was. It was just a matter of time.

***

It's been about three hours and twenty minutes since the death of the Aardvark. The reason I know is 'cause I can see the clock that hangs above Peterson and Rat Hole's cell. I'd just told Peterson the time when we got the news. It pisses me off, the way only one side of our floor can see the fucking clock. Everybody on the other side moans about how it annoys them, having to keep asking the time. Let me tell you something, it's more annoying having to yell the time across every five fucking seconds, I swear down. Anyway, I pull out a comic from under my mattress. I can tell Lewis has been reading it – or trying to read it - he's dog-eared the pages. If there's one thing that pisses me off – *one* fucking thing - it's people fucking with my comics.

'You been reading my comics?' I ask him.

He mutters something and rolls over, pretending to be asleep. Lewis has no respect for comics. He says things like, 'I wouldn't wipe my arse on them,' and then the next thing you know the bastard's reading one.

'Hey!' I say leaning across and jabbing him in the ribs. 'If you're gonna read my comics then quit dog-earing the pages.'

'Stupid comics,' he grunts. 'Anyone'd think you was twelve, the way you're always getting a hard-on over them comics.'

'Fuck-wit,' I mutter. He just ignores me. I decide to let it go. Now's not the time and besides, we have this argument everyday. After living with him for a year, I've learnt to accept that Lewis is a man who will never appreciate quality Japanese comics.

'Hey! Long John!' Bucky yells from across the way. 'Tell us the time.'

'Time to go home!' Lewis yells back. A few people on our side laugh. Nobody on their side laughs. On their side, they take the time *very* seriously.

'C'mon, man! Tell us the time!'

'Three twenty,' I yell back.

'Time you went to sleep!' Raymer yells from somewhere below.

'Time you went to sleep!' Peterson mimics him in the gayest voice you ever thought possible.

'I know who that was!' Raymer yells, taking his keys from his pocket and making for the stairs. 'I know who said that!'

***

It was yesterday. I was sitting at the dinner table with Bucky and a kid known as D.T, when I saw Whitey and Peterson approaching. They'd just picked up from the hatch and were making a beeline for our table. They sat down opposite me. I knew that Whitey wanted to talk to me. I wasn't with Lewis and he never sits with me if I'm not with Lewis.

'How's it goin'?' he asked, signalling for Bucky to pass the salt.

'Not bad,' I said. 'Yourself?'

'Okay.' He fixed me with a look. 'I noticed you're getting on with the Aardvark.' It didn't come as a surprise when he said this. I figured Peterson would have told him.

'I wouldn't say that,' I said. 'I mean, I spoke to him for a couple of seconds. It was about comics, that's all.'

They both laughed. 'You and your fuckin' comics,' Peterson said. 'Always beating off over them comics.'

'No big deal,' I muttered. 'You know me, I'll talk comics with anybody who'll give me the time.'

'Johnny,' Whitey said, looking suddenly serious. 'You know what he's in here for, don't you?'

'Course. I mean, don't get me wrong, man. The kid's scum.'

'He's a piece of shit and I'm gonna fucking nail him,' Whitey said, slamming the salt onto the table.

'Good,' I said, nodding enthusiastically, 'I'm lookin' forward to it.'

Whitey smiled when I said this. 'Yeah?'

'Course.'

'Good.' He leaned across the table and slapped me across the back. "Cause I want you to do something for me.'

'What?'

'Seeing as you two are such close friends, I want you to ask him for a game of pool. Tomorrow, in association.'

'Come again?'

He lowered his voice. 'I want you to get him away from the wardens. They always stand next to him. I need you to draw him away from them. That's the only way I'm gonna get a chance.'

'He won't buy it,' I said firmly. 'We only spoke for a few seconds. Ain't like he trusts me.'

'He trusts you enough to lend you his *rare* comic,' Peterson said.

Lewis, you fucking idiot! You and your fucking mouth!

'Just leave it a few days,' I said, thinking on my feet. 'It's raving. Raymer's watching his every move.'

'Raymer's on nights. It'll be Waters on the floor and Clarke and Henderson in the office.'

I shook my head. 'It won't work. Waters'll be watching him like a hawk. You'll get ten seconds. Tops.'

'Good.' He stood up and took a swig of his drink. 'Ten seconds is all it'll take.'

***

Ten seconds. In this place, a fight never gets past ten seconds. Ten seconds is all you get and you've gotta make it count. As I lay in my cell that night, I wondered what Whitey was planning. I wondered what Lewis had been saying and if Whitey didn't have it in for me as well. I wondered if Waters would suss what was going on and whether I'd get the blame for it. I knew I had to do it. In this place, you've gotta look after number one. Whitey was already pissed at me. I had to get back in his good books.

The following day we took association at two. England were playing Argentina and everybody was crowded round the telly. I had a medical so I got there a few minutes late. As I entered I spotted Whitey in the middle of the crowd. He gave me this look that told me not to approach him. I went and stood by Lewis. I'd decided that if Whitey didn't give me the signal, then I wouldn't do anything. I'd just watch the football, like everybody else.

Beckham had just sent it wide when D.T. came across and stood next to me.

'Johnny.'

'D.T. How's tricks?'

'Good. I heard you're gonna help Whitey nail the Aardvark.'

I didn't answer.

'Someone's gotta do it,' he said. 'Kid's an informer. He deserves it.'

'You'd best not fuck this up,' Lewis whispered. 'Just do as Whitey told you.'

Just then, Owen hit the post and the place went nuts.

As it was, I watched quite a bit of the game. At one point I thought that Whitey had changed his mind. We were forty minutes into the second half and Heskey had just taken the ball off Veron, when Rukus tapped me on the shoulder.

'Whitey wants you.'

I looked across at Whitey, who nodded at me. 'Ask him,' he mouthed.

As I moved away, Lewis tapped me on the shoulder.

'Go on, son,' he whispered. 'Fucking 'ave it.'

I walked over to where the Aardvark was standing and tapped his fist.

'How's it goin?'

'Good. Yerself?'

'Okay,' I said. 'Hey, thanks for the comic. It's fuckin' dark.'

'No problem.'

'Enjoying the game?'

'S'alright,' he said. 'I ain't really a fan, 'cept for when the World Cup's on.'

'Yeah, me too.'

'Heskey yoooou wanker!' Lewis started chanting.

'Behave!' Waters yelled.

'Hey, d'you fancy a game of pool?' I said. 'We can watch the match from over there.'

He looked up at Waters, who gave him a nod. 'Sure,' he said. 'I must warn you though, I ain't much of a pool player.'

I laughed, 'I ain't too hot myself.' We crossed to the table. I glanced over at Whitey. He had his eyes on Waters, which meant that Waters was watching me. 'You wanna break?'

'Don't mind.' He took the triangle from the rack and placed it on the felt. I glanced back at Whitey. He was moving through the crowd, his eyes still on Waters. The Aardvark was taking the balls out one at a time, dropping them into the triangle. 'We're missing the black,' he said. Out of the corner of my eye, I saw that Peterson was also on the move. He was heading in the other direction, towards Waters. I looked back at the Aardvark. He was on his knees, riddling his queue around in the shoot, trying to dislodge the missing ball. Whitey was approaching him from behind, all the while glancing across to see what Waters was doing. As he drew level, he reached into his pocket and pulled out a sock. In his other hand, he held the black ball.

It only took a second. Even if I was going to say something, I wouldn't have had time. Before I'd had a chance, Whitey had slipped the black ball into the sock and swung it; a short, fluid flick of the wrist, cracking the Aardvark round the back of the head as if he were cracking the top of an egg, sending his blood spattering across the table, staining the felt like oil.

The place erupted. Everyone knew what was happening.

The Aardvark slumped down, sliding from the table, onto the floor. I couldn't see him, but I figured that it was pretty severe. Whitey was putting the boot in, lifting his right leg up and stamping down repeatedly. Water's was blowing his whistle, pushing his way through the crowd. People were jostling each other, yelling their support, fighting for view. Rukus was up on the table, mimicking Whitey's every move, stomping on the felt with a look of fierce concentration. An alarm was ringing - the same alarm that went off when Jango got onto the roof - and suddenly, Clarke and two other wardens were there.

'263!' Waters was yelling. '263! Back off! Back off!' He made it to Whitey, had him by both arms and was dragging him away from the Aardvark. Whitey kept on kicking until he couldn't reach and then he was spitting and Clarke appeared and began to help Waters and between them, they managed to overpower him. The other wardens were yelling at us to stand back. Beckham scored a penalty against the Argies and we went through to the second phase. Not that anybody gave a fuck. The whole place was going mental. Everybody was fucking wired.

***

It's been a few hours since the death of the Ardvark, although none of us know when he actually died. For all we know, he could've been dead before the wardens pulled Whitey off him. We're just going on what the bulletin says. The time on it says twenty four hundred hours.

'What's that mean?' Lewis asked when we got it, peering over my shoulder.

'Midnight.'

'Sub,' he said, abruptly. 'Sub-je ...'

'Subject,' I read. 'Subject 292, Lee Finkle, has officially been declared dead. An investigation is under way in which you will all be required to cooperate.'

'Oh,' he said and threw himself onto his bed. 'What's that mean?'

'Means they're gonna ask us some questions.' He didn't respond. The whole wing was silent. Everybody was studying the bulletin.

'Looks like you've inherited this,' he said, picking up the X Files comic from the floor and laughing faintly, but I could tell that he didn't find it very funny either.

A couple of hours has passed since the bulletin went round. The clock opposite says three thirty. Whitey's cell's empty, which means that they've decided to question Danny Wire first. Wire shares a cell with Whitey. They probably figured he was in on it.

Somewhere below us, a door slides open. It's the main door. I can hear Raymer, in the recreation area. He's saying something about Waters and Clarke. Then there's the voice of a woman. As soon as she speaks, we all leap up off our beds and rush to get a look. Peterson wolf-whistles her and a few people laugh. Everybody's pressed up against their bars, trying to get a glimpse. She's not that fit, pretty old and wearing a suit. She's carrying a black folder. Me and Lewis watch her for a moment before I turn away and throw myself onto my bed.

'I'd still do her though,' Lewis says, as if debating it with himself. He climbs back onto his bed and we both lie there, staring up at the ceiling. The place has gone quiet again. Funny, but in a way, it feels like any other morning. Only difference is that everybody's awake. Ain't nobody gonna sleep tonight.

A Day Out

Eleanor Knight

'**O**h, all the things one can do in London in a single day!'
Hermione stood, her sensibly proportioned calves tapering,
not quite parallel, towards the grass from underneath her skirt.
Not a flattering length that, Margaret reflected. These days it
was hard to know what was. One wanted to hide one's worst
features of course but at the same time didn't want to look as
if one were trundling about on casters: just below the knee,
she'd stuck with that now for nearly a decade. It wasn't the
first time that Margaret had looked at her new friend and been
reminded of an Aunt Sally. It was Hermione's height,
combined with her not stoutness exactly but substance, yes
one could get away with calling it that, and an habitual
expression of mild shock, which Margaret now recognised as a
lusty enthusiasm for novelty worn on a face whose golden age
had been the era of heavy powder and eyeshadow in kingfisher
blue. Not for the first time either had Margaret found herself
regarding Hermione from the feet up. If she were in a
fairground, she wondered, how hard would she have to try to
knock her down?

They were by the lake in St James's Park. Hermione,
standing on an area of grass she had declared safe to patronise,
it being clear of goose shit, gazed across the lake towards
Buckingham Palace, discreetly hidden from view behind the
great net curtain drawn by the morning haze. Margaret knelt
beside her friend, unpacking the elements of a brunch
(Hermione seemed incapable of saying the word snack) from a
carrier bag. She had been unable to resist two dear little *quiches
lorraines*, inviolate inside twin plastic bubbles on the

supermarket's orderly shelf. There were two cartons of fresh pink grapefruit juice, each with its own straw and (wasn't she marvellous) she had brought along in her handbag a thermos of good, hot tea brewed properly at 7 o'clock that morning in an earthenware teapot which she had placed on the warm spot where the kitchen worktop ran over the boiler, while two sparrows titivated themselves in the little stone birdbath outside the window, cleaning their feathers in the few remaining droplets of a light rain that had fallen overnight on Haywards Heath.

Margaret drew the line at plastic cutlery and had managed to slip a couple of large silver forks from her wedding set into her bag alongside the flask, half wondering if they could be classed as offensive weapons were she ever to be interrogated on the matter, under what circumstances she couldn't imagine. Thank the Lord that the Major's penknife ('Be prepared!') had not been inside his breast pocket that day. She wouldn't have wanted a violent death for her husband, not even by accident, when it was too late anyway. She placed the forks on top of a couple of white paper napkins on the grass, where they flashed brilliantly in the sun.

A pelican emerged from the shrubs on Duck Island and hung its wings out speculatively. A hasty little coot zigzagged across the water for no other reason than that it could. The roar of the traffic was nothing but a distant grumble beyond the Mall and the band of Her Majesty's Household Cavalry were coming to the end of an open air rehearsal of Men of Harlech across the road behind them. If this was what Hermione called slumming it, she could happily never go shopping again.

The flag was up. 'On a day like today, I wonder if one couldn't live one's entire life all at once. A blue sky can be so invigorating. Always dangerous to suggest that sort of thing to Mrs Woolf, as I remember; it got me into terrible trouble. Still, poor dear, she was a bit down in the dumps, you know. A nice bit of rice pudding put her right.'

Hermione would keep talking until she, Margaret, played the game. It was evidently another of Hermione's untruths, which Margaret enjoyed far too much to call lies and thus risk their permanent censure. Lies sounded spiteful;

rather, for Hermione, they seemed to function as a navigational tool. She was rudderless, like an outlandish character in one of those novels that Margaret could never quite believe in, who had no friends or dependents and therefore was free to engage with the world in a purely egotistical way, though granted it was more interesting than romance. She knew who this Woolf character would turn out to be, given their location, but she wasn't going to acknowledge it.

'Rice pudding?'

'Well of course, I couldn't very well call her Virginia in those days. Yes. She was awfully fond of what I call wet foods. They all were, the Bloomsburys.' On her lips the word sounded like a variety of fruit yoghurt. '*Consommé*, various things *en daube*, if you remember what that was. We ate the leftovers, naturally, down in the kitchen. So much soup. Mother said we'd all float away... I suppose she was right in the end. Lovely little Scottie called Clarissa. Lively little thing.'

Hermione had the look in her eyes of a racehorse that has just shaken off its rider. She knew she had strayed too far off course and badly wanted reining in.

'Hermione, you mentioned a project.'

Hermione clapped her hands together as if bringing herself to order and sat down with relief beside Margaret on the grass.

'Ah yes. Let's watch the world go by and I'll tell you all about it. Aren't you marvellous!'

Margaret demurred as she poured the steaming tea into two cups, one stainless steel, one plastic, and handed the stainless steel one to Hermione.

'Star-crossed lovers,' said Hermione. 'I've been thinking about it since I found you that day...' They both of them only ever referred to it as 'that day...', Margaret because she couldn't trust herself to say 'the day my husband died' without the awful lead ball of grief rolling up from the deep pit inside herself, and Hermione because no other day they referred to between themselves could possibly match it for significance.

'Chance meetings. I'm wondering if they're nothing to do with chance at all.'

'How do you mean?'

'What I mean,' she said with a schoolmarmish emphasis that was almost involuntary, 'is that there may be reasons you or I have not yet grasped for our meeting. I'm talking about other forces.'

'Oh, the supernatural,' said Margaret, hoping to hide her disappointment. 'I'm not sure I go in for all that.'

'In a way,' said Hermione, picking up a fork and eyeing the quiches. Margaret obligingly popped them out from their spheres and served them up in the foil cases.

'I've been reading up on it, the influence of the planets and all that. Mmm. Glorious pie. I'm more and more convinced that there must be something in it.'

'The fault, dear Brutus, lies not in our stars but in ourselves that we are underlings' said Margaret, prodding at a sliver of decorative bacon.

'I've never thought of myself as an underling.'

'What I mean is I don't believe in astrology.' To Margaret's mind, although she wouldn't now volunteer the information to Hermione, there was nothing worse than women of a certain age, an age which she realised with alarm now coincided with her own, oohing and aahing over horoscopes; women with very little experience of life outside the domestic sphere claiming that because they were a Gemini they'd be a better wife to the Taurean Laurence Olivier than the troublesome Scorpio Joan Plowright, and she was the second after all. No, it was all gossip and tittle tattle and the kind of people who went in for it usually worried about the acquisition of paper doilies. She was shocked at Hermione.

'I'm afraid I was brought up an Anglican.'

'Yes of course you were. Now, let me tell you about the central line of totality.'

'As you wish.' Totality was a ghastly word. It was surely one of those meaningless Americanisms, like potentiality. And Hermione was smiling one of those patronising smiles that professional psychics use on members of the established church.

'Margaret I wish you wouldn't look so lumpen.'

'I'm so sorry. I didn't mean to be rude. The grass is a bit damp still, that's all. Do go on.' She would, of course.

'The central line of totality, that's the line along which we can expect a total eclipse of the sun to be visible, passes through parts of Devon and Cornwall. Here we will have about four percent of the sun remaining in view, as it were, though of course we won't be looking directly at it. The thing is that the London Chamber of Commerce – don't look like that, you've heard of them – have predicted that in the two minutes we all spend standing still for the eclipse, the country will lose five hundred million pounds in business. If that's not a significant event, I don't know what is. They don't make those kind of predictions about the Cenotaph.'

'It's on a Sunday.'

'Alright, that bit is. But you don't get a warning from the City splashed all over the Evening Standard before Armistice Day, do you?'

'But they wouldn't. It's not as if anyone observes it much these days and besides, it would seem terribly disrespectful. And ungrateful.'

They both became thoughtful for a moment, Hermione dredging the remains of her grapefruit juice as quietly as she could and Margaret turning to look for something in her handbag.

'But look. You and I meeting, a death – sorry, your loss.' Hermione squeezed the carton in her hand and looked about for a litter bin. 'Your loss was my gain, you might say.'

If this was going to be some sort of declaration, Margaret would have to pretend to be taken ill very suddenly so as not to have to hear it. What if Hermione had hidden a lifetime of emotional savings under a mattress and had chosen today, on a whim, to put the lot into a carpet bag and pour it out onto her counter as if she were a small provincial building society? She was suddenly back at school, with another girl asking to be her best friend. It was a transaction she'd always found pathetic. Hermione certainly was tactless.

'I'm going to start combing the newspapers for significant events. God knows I've been involved in many of them over the years' she said, smoothing her hair behind her ears. Margaret was not taking the bait. 'I'm going to put together a sort of millennial scrap book. I'll be looking for things that are truly out of the ordinary, not just murder and robberies and so forth, but things that would really make your eyes pop. Now I've let you in on it, you can let me know if you spot anything.'

'Is that it?'

'What?'

'Is that your project?'

'Don't you like it?'

Margaret didn't know whether to be relieved or disappointed. 'I – the line of totality. I got a bit lost there.'

'Not to worry,' said Hermione rising to her feet. 'It's not important really. It's the principle. Which paper do you read?'

Margaret named it. Hermione made a face. 'Then we shan't overlap. Jolly good.'

While they were talking, the pelican had waded out from Duck Island and perched itself on top of the white railings at the bottom of the bank. Now it tipped itself clumsily off and began waddling up towards them with a world weary calm.

'Ugly aren't they?' said Hermione. 'You know the medievals used to think that the young killed the father and that the mother fought the little nippers to the death, shed her own blood and then dribbled it over the babies to bring them back to life again – a sort of redemptive unguent if you like. Patricide, infanticide, attempted matricide. No, one wouldn't have wanted to be a pelican in those days.'

'I've always hated their eyes,' said Margaret, bristling. They look as if they know something we don't.'

'He's getting rather close. I hope he doesn't understand English; he may hold it against us. They were a gift from the Russian Ambassador you know.'

'Oh. Very well then.' Margaret addressed the pelican. '*Doh-bray-yu oo-tra. Vih ga-var-ee-tyeh pa-an-glee-ski?* My husband was very know thine enemy. I can do it in Mandarin, too.'

The pelican advanced, rolling heavily from side to side.

'He's rather supercilious isn't he?' said Hermione. 'Barristers used to look like that before they all got very young and started spending most of their time in the gym. Now

Vino's has gone as well. Those were the days. Shoo!' The bird stopped for a moment, staring blankly at them. 'Shoo!'

'I don't think he's listening. Could you be a bit more pelican? You're sounding like a barn owl.'

The pelican started off again and in a couple of heavy steps its head was level with Margaret's.

'Ugh' said Hermione. 'Look at its throat. It's like a bag made of human skin.'

'I suppose that's what mine would look like if you took it all off. Wrinkled and bobbly. It's just the wrong side of see-through. Oh do go away you horrid bird!' Margaret flapped at it as if she were swotting a wasp.

The pelican made a lunge for the forks in Margaret's hand and with a sudden snap of its hard, clapperboard bill, had them jangling together in its pendulous maw. One of them landed sideways, forcing the skin to stretch right across and three small, hideous protrusions were all that could be seen of the tines. The other bobbed about with its handle just visible above the rim of the bird's bill, glinting in the sunshine.

'I think I'm going to be sick,' said Hermione.

'Don't be silly. We'll just have to get them out.'

'I don't think I can, that horrible skin sack thing.'

'If we don't get them out, the poor thing might swallow them. It would be a lot worse than swallowing a fishbone.'

'They swallow things whole all the time!'

'Not forks. Now, if we can just …'

'I can't get my hand near that thing – look at its eyes!'

'Oh for goodness' sake, Hermione. You're a trained nurse!'

She had her there. Neither of them could admit that this was a lie as they would have to face the profoundly uncomfortable thought that someone with no professional medical associations had manhandled Major Reynolds that day into the back of a black cab while he was still possibly a little bit alive.

'Yes, yes!' said Hermione, 'But I was never a vet. I'm not sure even a vet …'

'Hermione!' Margaret took charge of the situation. 'I want my forks back. They were a wedding present and I will not allow them to be eaten by a pelican. Neither do I wish them to do harm, however revolting this wretched bird might be.'

She made a grab for its beak, causing the bird to blunder heavily into Hermione's legs while flapping its wings in alarm.

'Ugh! It's like a dead weight, except that it's all warm and feathery.'

The bird swung its head miserably to and fro.

'That's what crocodiles do with their prey. Wave it around like that,' said Margaret, moving closer. She was almost enjoying herself. She had forgotten how calm and purposeful she could become in a crisis. She pushed up one sleeve of her jacket and decided not to unfasten her wristwatch. 'Hermione, try and sort of buffet it over here as best you can.'

'I'm sorry Margaret, I can't bear it. I've never thought of them as living things before. It's like a horrid nightmare come alive. Its feathers are all hard.'

The pelican shifted its bulk from one scaly leg to the other, agitated, like a boxer in the ring wondering where the next punch was going to land, and who was going to land it. The forks joggled about hopelessly in its horrible mouth. Margaret reached her bare forearm towards it but it startled and made as if to peck and in doing so lodged the second fork further down inside. It started to make a weird guttural, whistling sound.

'Oh dear. The poor thing! Would you believe it, there's still nobody about. Surely somebody must come into the park eventually. Time's getting on.'

The haze had lifted now, or had been burned off by the sun, which fell in bright story-book dapples through the leaves of the plane trees and onto the grass. Margaret cast a glance along the length of the park towards the palace end, keeping the pelican within her sights. This wasn't difficult as Hermione's frankly ridiculous flapping about had terrified the poor bird and it was swaying about in a disturbed fashion, quite understandably. She felt rather disturbed herself. Who else ought to be here? Men of Harlech had ceased some minutes ago and then there had been a bit of shouting and they'd all disappeared. Dogwalkers? No, they would have all left hours ago. The people who put out the deckchairs wouldn't have started yet, and anyway they were way down the other end by the bandstand. The little wooden booths selling refreshments were surely staffed, but noone would be looking this way. She had once spotted a member of the Cabinet taking a shortcut through here, deep in conversation with someone she assumed must be an advisor of some sort, but she doubted whether the business of government could be interrupted for the removal of cutlery from wildfowl. She made one more attempt. Surprising herself and Hermione (in celebration of which she raised a glass of whisky to herself eleven hours later and patted her lap for the cat to join her on the sofa) Margaret stared into the angry eye of the pelican and plunged her hand straight into its mouth. The pelican beat its wings furiously, shedding tufts of grubby dry down onto the grass at their feet, twisting its neck and forcing Margaret to follow with her arm in its mouth as if salvaging a spoon dropped in a mixing bowl. Margaret tugged as gently as she could at the fork that lay horizontally and freed the prongs from the bird's gullet. Then, before Hermione could offer weakly to help, she had both forks out and was looking about for a napkin to wipe them on. They smelled strongly of fish.

The pelican closed its mouth with a smack like a slapstick, stood its ground for a moment, and then turned and lumbered back towards the lake.

It was so kind of Hermione to walk her to the platform. Rush hour had crept up on them somehow, despite the afternoon being disappointing. Hermione had been right this morning about how much one could do in a day and Margaret was now so exhausted she wondered if she hadn't in fact spent a lifetime in the stifling galleries of the Royal Academy for what her companion had billed as the Old Bags' Summer Matinée: too much to look at in too little space and far too many people in the way. Hermione had likened it to a car boot sale, within she was sure, the earshot of several academicians and their entourages. 'They surely can't *all* be,' said Hermione, opening the door of the Members' Tea Room to find every table full and a queue that looked as though it were there to stay. Margaret had said not to worry there were plenty of less salubrious places on the way to the station where one could get a cup of tea without being surrounded by the elderly.

It wasn't the pelican that had upset her, although she was now struggling to remember if there was an old wives' tale about not taking cutlery out of the house: no, she had done her best in that situation. The shock had been witnessing her friend's instant transmutation from capability in solid form to twittering old woman. While the Major was alive, he and Margaret had trundled alongside each other for years and, apart from the self-conscious, self-effacing references to middle-age spread, grey hairs and things not being what they used to be, they had always, she believed, retained the familiar aura of their youth. But here was someone her own age, a stranger effectively, whom she was forced to look at in the same way as any other, putting them into the correct boxes for age, sex, appearance. It was an evolutionary game that kept one in one's peer group. At a base level, she supposed, it prevented unproductive alliances between young girls and their old headmasters, for example. It prevented one from going to discotheques at sixty-five. In short it was only natural, and it was therefore only natural that the time Margaret spent with Hermione made her feel old.

'At least we're going in the same direction as everyone else,' shouted Hermione through the moving maze of suits and briefcases. People walked so fast through the crush that Margaret was tempted to lift both feet off the concourse to see how far she would be borne along.

'PICKPOCKETS AND TICKET TOUTS ARE OPERATING IN THIS STATION.' The public address system was just another element of bustle to be ignored, together with the strong aroma of coffee at five minutes past six in the evening, the soup stalls, sweets, flowers, newspapers, more coffee, ties, handbags; there was a great deal more money to be made out of people getting on or off a train than there was once they were actually travelling on it.

'Margaret?'

'Here I am.' Margaret reappeared at Hermione's side as they reached the grimy concrete overhang that signalled the entrance to platforms 9 to 15.

'There, you see? No more than a handful of people coming this way. Only one poor soul coming from your platform. I could never come home to a place that shared its name with a railway station. No wonder Vanessa and the rest of them made such a thing about Bloomsbury. One could hardly have called them the Eustons.'

Quite unexpectedly, Margaret found herself kissing Hermione warmly on both cheeks. Hermione looked mildly surprised but not displeased.

'Lovely day. Don't get squashed on the way out!'

Margaret turned towards her train and almost collided with the bouncy little man in denims coming off the platform. He looked kind.

'Home at last eh?' he said, squeezing past.

'Yes,' she said, the long day closing behind her like a book. 'Home at last.'

I'm Reviewing a Play at the Albany and I was Wondering if You'd Like to Come Along

Luke Kennard

Charles Thornton was a stenographer. A stenographer is someone who takes notes in shorthand or operates a shorthand machine. I didn't know that until I happened upon in it in a dictionary, but Charles had known it all his adult life. When he was 11 he received a vision informing him, among other things, that he would become a stenographer. He began working towards it right away, saving up his errand money for a second-hand stenograph and subscribing to *Junior Stenographer* magazine, a monthly journal published and printed in Canada. At fourteen he took his first stenography exam and passed with the highest mark the examining board had ever seen (94%). There was a story in his local paper about it, but it is too boring to include here. Soon after that he started working as a stenographer's assistant at Bartleby Throws, a legal firm in the city. For two years he wore a ¾ size suit and tie and, in the evenings to wind-down, played a ¾ size cello.

Charles was also a theatre critic, but it didn't pay much and was really more of a sideline. By the age of thirty-three, Charles was Stenographer in Chief for Sing, Sing & Beard – which was pretty good. He was in love with a woman named Madison Piper, head of Sales Received for Sing, Sing & Beard. She was 5' 6", blonde and often wore a black flower in her hair.

This is important as it happened in Charles's past: when he was nine he walked into the bathroom and found his babysitter, a seventeen year old girl named Petula, standing naked in front of the bathroom mirror, humming a tune he sort of recognised. 'Hi Charles,' she said. Charles walked back out of the bathroom and sat down at his desk where he practised writing in shorthand.

One Tuesday morning in Spring, after two years working for Sing, Sing & Beard, Charles found Madison at the water buffalo, drinking glass after glass of ice cold water. Madison Piper was a woman of remarkable thirst.

'Good morning,' said Charles, 'I'm reviewing a play at the Albany and I was wondering if you'd like to come along.' He handed Madison the Albany's Spring brochure.

> Saturday, April 23rd, 7:30pm – Chase Bullmori's *'The Sausage and I'*.
>
> *'The Sausage and I'* is a play after the epic tradition for five actors (all sausages). The sausages are tied to invisible thread and jiggled around in order to simulate movement and dialogue. It is a silent play. After the performance, Chase Bullmori discusses the inspiration behind the piece.
>
> Bullmori's past works, *'The Parchment'* and *'Eponymous Milk'*, were both nominated for Bonesong Awards for Innovation and his first collection of poetry, *'Poems'*, is published this year by Charlie Horse Books.
>
> This is the first British production of *'The Sausage and I'* – which premiered at the Oslo Theatre Festival in 2002. "The challenge," said Bullmori, in interview with P. S. McFadden, "was wringing tragedy from the situation. When I told most people the premise behind *'The Sausage and I'*, they laughed out loud – but those same people left the theatre weeping."
>
> Adults £13, Concessions £8. The play is not suitable for young children and contains strobe effects.

'I'm not sure,' said Madison. 'I don't really like experimental theatre.'

'Oh, it's not experimental as such,' said Charles. 'I've seen his other plays – Bullmori's narratives are actually pretty traditional.'

'It sounds lovely,' said Madison Piper. 'But I have an awful lot of work to do on the Bird Index.'

'In that case,' said Charles, 'I'm just going to ask you over and over again until you say yes.'

And with that Charles asked Madison Piper if she wanted to accompany him to the theatre. She laughed – and Charles asked her again. He wouldn't stop, even when Madison poured a glass of ice cold water over his head. He followed her into her office and continued to ask her if she wanted to accompany him to the theatre. Madison explained that such behaviour was unacceptable as it was tantamount to harassment and, when two hours later Charles hadn't stopped asking her to accompany him to the theatre, decided to take legal advice.

'Would you describe his tone as "stridulous"?' asked Madison's lawyer, Mr. Haycock.

'I'm not sure,' said Madison, holding the phone to one ear and putting her hand over the other.

'For the sake of argument,' said Haycock, 'we'll call it "stridulous".'

'I'm reviewing a play at the Albany and I was wondering if you'd like to come along,' said Charles.

'It's really annoying,' said Madison.

'Good,' said Haycock, 'that's very good. Try to suffer as much as possible.'

'I'm reviewing a play at the Albany and I was wondering if you'd like to come along,' said Charles.

'I don't know,' said Madison, 'I might just go to the play with him.'

'On no account should you agree to go to the play with him,' said Haycock. 'At this stage in proceedings it would be very damaging to your case. You wouldn't even get a hearing. You're going to have to tough it out, Maddy. And if you suffer a breakdown, all the better. That would be very good for your case. I recommend that you speak to your doctor. Tough it out.'

Madison called her doctor.

'I'm reviewing a play at the Albany and I was wondering if you'd like to come along,' said Charles.

'I need to speak to Dr. Blend,' she told Dr. Blend's receptionist. 'It's an emergency.'

Dr. Blend was an Eastern European G.P. with very little to add to this story. He suggested booking an appointment for later in the week.

'Geeze,' said Haycock. 'You sort of have to admire his persistence.'

'No you don't,' said Madison.

'I'm reviewing a play at the Albany and I was wondering if you'd like to come along,' said Charles.

'For the love of God,' cried Madison.

'Call me tomorrow,' said Haycock. 'I'm interested to see how this plays out. I'll look into a few relevant cases this evening.'

Madison's conversation with Haycock cost her in the region of £500, but it was worth it as he was a lawyer.

At six o' clock, Charles Thornton followed Madison Piper to her car, asking if she would like to accompany him to the theatre. When Madison unlocked her car, Charles got into the passenger seat and said, 'I'm reviewing a play at the Albany and I was wondering if you'd like to come along.'

After they had eaten together, Madison took a bath, surrounded by candles. Charles sat outside the bathroom door of Madison's apartment, saying, 'I'm reviewing a play at the Albany and I was wondering if you'd like to come along.'

All night, Charles sat by Madison's bedside, whispering, 'I'm reviewing a play at the Albany and I was wondering if you'd like to come along.' Madison fell asleep at two a.m.

The next day, Charles stood outside Madison's bedroom door while she dressed and put a black flower in her hair.

Madison drove Charles to work and bought him a large coffee from a drive-through cafe.

'There you go,' she said. 'Enjoy your fucking coffee.'

'I'm reviewing a play at the Albany and I was wondering if you'd like to come along,' said Charles.

'Hey kid,' said Haycock, on the phone. 'What's the state of play?'

'He hasn't left my side since yesterday.'

'You let him into your *house*?'

'I tried to shut him out,' said Madison, 'but he started weeping. The sound of him wondering if I'd like to accompany him to the theatre through his tears was too much to bear.'

'So you let him into your *house*?'

'Mark, please don't start repeating things.'

'You let him into your *house*?' said Haycock and laughed. 'I'm just messing with you,' he said. 'Ha ha ha. Did he become violent?'

'No,' said Madison.

'I'm reviewing a play at the Albany and I was wondering if you'd like to come along,' said Charles.

'I don't think he slept at all,' she said.

'Listen to this,' said Haycock. 'In 1988 a man was fined £75,000 for yelling at a tree.'

'I'm sorry?' said Madison.

'That's the closest I could find,' said Haycock. 'And the details are kind of patchy. The guy pleaded insanity so they had to prove that he wasn't mad – and they managed it, somehow. He wasn't mad at all. Only way you can get away with yelling at a tree is if you're nuts. Here's the weird part: he pays his fine – he was a pretty well-off guy – he pays his fine and two weeks later they find him yelling at the same tree again, only this time even louder. He was tried again, pleaded insanity, and this time it turned out he *was* insane. Spent the rest of his life in a secure institution yelling at a goddamned tree.'

'That doesn't strike me as relevant,' said Madison.

'I'm reviewing a play at the Albany and I was wondering if you'd like to come along,' said Charles.

'Is this guy Charles insane, do you think?' said Haycock.

'I don't know,' said Madison.

'Have you seen your doctor yet?'

'I haven't had a breakdown yet,' said Madison.

'It's probably in your interest to have the breakdown as soon as possible,' said Haycock. 'The sooner you have it, the sooner we can proceed with the prosecution.'

'I'll see what I can do.'

'Call me tomorrow with an update,' said Haycock. Madison placed the phone back on the receiver.

'Lets go for lunch,' she said to Charles.

'I'm reviewing a play at the Albany and I was wondering if you'd like to come along,' said Charles.

That afternoon Madison Piper had an important meeting with her colleagues and superiors at which she was to give a presentation. She tried to explain this to Charles, but his only response was to wonder aloud whether she wanted to accompany him to the theatre. The meeting was not a complete disaster as her colleagues and superiors took Charles to be part of the act.

That night Madison took Charles for dinner at *Montgomery's*. They had three bottles of red wine and stayed for cocktails.

'You did *what?*' said Haycock.

'Nothing happened,' said Madison. 'He just lay next to me, whispering, *I'm reviewing a play at the Albany and I was wondering if you'd like to come along*, until he fell asleep. He looked so awful, sitting in that uncomfortable chair by my bed, his eyes all bloodshot.'

'This isn't going to stand up too well in court,' said Haycock. 'Neither is your buying him dinner. Do you have the receipts?'

'He has to *eat.*'

'I'm reviewing a play at the Albany and I was wondering if you'd like to come along,' said Charles.

'If you have the receipts, burn them. How are you coming along with the breakdown?'

'Not great.'

'Are you trying to destroy me, Maddy? I was telling your story to Rube last night and he gave me the Tanning case – Rube worked on the Tanning case years ago. This Tanning decides he wants to write a novel about a colleague of his – so he starts writing down everything the guy says. Whenever he opens his mouth, there's Tanning, waiting to write it down. Drove the poor guy crazy.'

'What happened?'

'It's actually a pretty good novel. But Tanning got five years for fraud in a completely unrelated matter. And the other guy, I don't know. Once he'd recovered he tried to write a novel about Tanning in response, but it sort of flopped. The whole Tanning wave had peaked.'

The line went dead.

'I'm reviewing a play at the Albany and I was wondering if you'd like to come along,' said Charles.

'Okay,' said Madison. 'I'll come to the stupid sausage play.'

***

The dialogue between the sausages, manifesting only as jiggling movements, was noted in the programme.

sausage2:   [Your attempt on my life has backfired.]
sausage1:   [I was raised in a pit of snakes.]
sausage2:   [When I found you I threw in more snakes.]
sausage1:   [I'm reviewing a play at the Albany and I was wondering if you'd like to come along.]

In the interval Madison drank a slightly off-chill glass of white wine with Charles Thornton in the theatre courtyard. The sun was setting over the grey apartment blocks and Charles hadn't said a word since she'd agreed to go to the play with him.

Somebody tapped her on the shoulder. She turned. Hey kid,' said Haycock. 'If I'd known it was Bullmori, I'd have taken you myself. Is this Charles?'

'Hi,' said Charles.

'Good for you,' said Haycock, patting Charles on the back. 'I knew you'd get her sooner or later.'

Haycock had greyed since the last time Madison had seen him. He drank a champagne cocktail from a highball glass and his tie depicted the surface of the moon.

'How are you enjoying the play?' he asked.

'It's the dumbest thing I've ever seen,' said Madison.

The Do-Gooders

Lauri Kubuitsile

I suppose I knew all along that we were poor. I put it down to the nonsense of the adults more than anything else. But I blame the do-gooders on my sister who made us a target for them in the first place. They'd been scouting us ever since we lived in the cottage on the lake with a hundred cats and René decided she wanted to go to church.

We weren't church people. At least not the churches of the Protestants with their tame white walls and bloodless Jesus. If we went to church at all, it was to the Catholic Church where the sun shone through the gory pictures of suffering in the windows and at the front, watching over it all, was the real Jesus, with sharp thorns poking into his head and blood dripping into his sorrow-filled eyes. The Catholic Church was about suffering. René's church was all about finding someone to help, whether they wanted it or not.

It all started that summer on the lake. When I look back I suppose I shouldn't blame René. She was fifteen years old and being fifteen she was busy looking for a boyfriend and decided that Jimmy Reynolds, the protestant minister's son, would be a good target. So Jimmy Reynolds came out to the lake and rowed about in the boat my mother stole from next door.

Jimmy didn't see the situation very clearly, at least not right away. Living on the lake with a boat and a hundred cats looks even a bit posh to an untrained eye. Besides, he was still distracted by René's newly grown breasts that filled out the cups of the red bikini she'd bought at K-Mart.

My mother wasn't happy about the whole thing. 'I don't trust a boy who's so clean,' she told René, her green eyes squeezed up into mean-guy slits. My mother was used to my brother Mike, who didn't bathe during school holidays unless swimming counted, and everyone knew it didn't. 'Besides,' she said, blowing perfect smoke rings out of her fire-engine red lipstick covered lips, 'you must watch out for those Protestants. They just take life too easy. Way too easy.'

René spouted back, 'I'll do what I want. Anyways, there's nothing you can do, I've already joined their church.'

A quiet hush filled the one room cement cottage while we waited for my mother to blow. The only noise was the whine of Felix, giving birth to the third litter of kittens born that summer. My mother kept silent, always something to fear, and René slammed out the screen door. The summer progressed with my mother's unresolved silence lingering in the humid air.

At that point in our lives, me and René and Mike were living with my mother and had been for about two years. My father was somewhere we didn't quite know, but when my mother had a few too many 'black days' he'd come back and pack us up and take us away to his place. His place changed a lot depending on his latest girlfriend. Last time his place was Barbara's place. She was okay if you like tight pink dresses, curlers and red nails. I didn't. René loved Barbara, who taught her how to pluck her eyebrows into surprised curves and to paint her toenails without getting nail polish on her skin. When we left, René cried for a whole week.

We moved to the cottage by the lake when school closed in June. We moved for the same reason we always did: my mother didn't pay the rent and we were evicted. The law was that you could only be evicted if you failed to pay rent for three months, so normally we stayed in a place just over three months when we lived with my mother. In a way, I liked it. I didn't waste time making friends and trying to fit in anywhere because I knew that we'd be leaving. René was always tearing bits of her heart off and leaving them behind. Her crying christened every new house.

We sailed through the summer. My mother ignored René's comings and goings; she was too busy with the cats anyway. We found most of them there. The cottage had been abandoned for many years and the cats had taken up residence. Others might have chased them but my mother, a victim of one too many evictions herself, refused. Mike and I loved it.

We'd never had pets before. Though most of the cats were too wild to catch, the baby kittens could be trapped in a corner and grabbed up. They hissed and spat and clawed us up and down our arms, but eventually if we held them enough they'd calm down. By the end of summer, some were even purring next to our heads on the pillow when we fell asleep at night.

One evening as the sun was sinking under the edge of the lake and we were sitting out on the rickety pier, a car pulled up. A tall man in ironed shorts and a collared golf shirt and his tiny wife in a pastel sweater set got out and came walking towards us. They stopped at the edge of the pier and the man spoke. 'Can I ask what you're doing here?'

My mother looked up from the kittens on her lap. 'Why of course you can. It's a free country, or so I've heard.' She went back to petting the cats.

The man looked at his wife who clung a bit tighter on his muscled arm. 'This is private property. It belongs to the Millers down in Chicago and I believe that boat you've got tied to the pier is ours.'

'Well is it now? You shouldn't leave your boat floating in the water untied, could get lost forever. You should be thanking us instead of accusing us of theft,' my mother lied. We actually took the boat out of their boathouse after my mother broke the rusty lock with a brick. 'As for this cottage, have you spoken to the Millers lately?'

The man was obviously not used to dealing with someone like my mother, few were. 'Well no, but I do know he never rents this place out.'

'Well, do ya now?' my mother handed me the kittens and stood up to her 5'9' height, all long legs, curly amber hair and green piercing eyes, and walked towards the man and his whimpering wife. Inches from the man's now level face she said, 'I think you oughta talk to Mr. Miller before ya come shooting your mouth off. People do change their minds.' Then she walked toward the cottage, shouting uncharacteristically mother-like, 'You kids better come on in now - the mosquitoes are biting.'

The next day the police car showed up. My mother talked to them for a bit at the driveway and then came back to the cottage and started packing things up. 'Go and call René. We're moving into town.'

René had seen the police car and knew what was happening. When I found her, she was crying into Jimmy Reynolds' shoulder. 'Mom says you gotta come and help pack.' It was okay by me because it was getting too cold in the damp cottage and school would be starting soon. The only sad part was leaving the cats. In the end though, we kept one, all black with white paws, who we named Mr. Mittens. Mike hid him in his backpack, keeping him quiet by wrapping his mouth with cellotape. We'd been living a week at the gray house in town before anyone knew he even had it.

I don't know how, but we managed to stay at the gray house most of the rest of the year. Although against my normal policy, I started to make a few friends at school. My best friend was a chubby girl called Veronicah. She lived in a big house near school. Sometimes I'd go there and her mother would give us cookies and we'd play with Veronicah's dollhouse.

But winter was coming and I could tell we were heading for trouble. My mother could be fun, a lot of fun, but when she started putting her Englebert Humperdink records on and sitting at the kitchen table smoking one cigarette after another, we all knew she was moving towards a black mood and we'd soon have to find my father to save us. I only hoped that she'd wait until Christmas because Veronicah and I had agreed to swap presents and I already knew what I would buy her. I'd seen it at the supermarket. A rhinestone tiara and little plastic shoes with rhinestones glued across the top. I knew she'd love them.

Thanksgiving weekend arrived and René had bought a turkey. She woke up early and had the turkey in the oven before anyone else got up. At 11:00, my mother still in bed, I heard a knock at the door. I was in the kitchen peeling potatoes as instructed by René. Mike shouted, 'Daddy's here!'

I left the potatoes to see who was at the door. At first I was confused. It was a crowd of people and at the front were Pastor Reynolds and Jimmy. People were holding boxes and grocery bags. They were smiling and I wasn't sure what they wanted. Then in the crowd I saw Veronicah and her cookie-giving mother and a man who I thought must be her father.

Then René said, 'Well Pastor Reynolds, isn't that so kind of you.' She started taking the packages and I realised that they were full of food, tins of vegetables, bags of potatoes, another turkey. I watched as the boy who sat in front of me in class set down a huge tin of yams and then the janitor from school patted me and Mike on the head before setting down a box of old clothes.

And then Veronicah was there. I couldn't look at her. Her mother spoke and I heard nothing. I wanted to cry and scream and hide myself away forever. How could they do this to me? To us? How could René smile now that we were the 'poor people'? How could Veronicah want to be my friend anymore? Why would she want some stupid plastic tiara and shoes from the 'poor girl'? Was that why her mother gave me cookies?

They left just before my mother woke up. 'What the hell is this?' she said to René pointing at all of the stuff piled up on the table.

'It's from the church. They wanted to help,' René tried.

One by one my mother picked things from the boxes. I remember the first was a bottle of beetroot salad, which she smashed against the white tiles across the kitchen. The purple red juice splattered spectacularly. Tins hit furniture, bottles broke windows, potatoes rolled under the couch.

'Fuck your church!' she screamed, breathing hard and turning to René, and with one quick flick of the back of her hand René fell to the kitchen floor, her hand cut on a broken jar. My mother turned and disappeared into the icy Thanksgiving morning, no shoes, no coat, still in her nightgown.

I wrapped René's hand in a dish towel and called the phone number my father had given me when we left last time. He arrived in what seemed a very short time and we left the house without packing a thing.

The next time we saw my mother it was six or seven years after the do-gooders. She looked different, older and sadder. We never lived with her again, though.

I think about that day of the do-gooders sometimes. I wonder what happened to René's turkey that was in the oven and Mike wonders about Mr. Mittens. But René has never mentioned it again.

No Trumpets Needed

Michael Morpurgo

I am a cameraman. I work freelance, working on my own. It's how I like it. I was on the West Bank a few weeks ago, my first job in the bitter cauldron of contention that is the Middle East. Of course I had seen on television, like most of us, the anguish of the grieving, the burnt out buses, the ritual humiliation at checkpoints, the tanks in the streets, the stone-throwing crowds, the olive groves and the hill-top settlements, children playing in open sewers in the refugee camps – and now, the wall. I knew the place in images, I was there to make more of them, I suppose. But I had a more personal reason for being there too. I saw it on television, watched in disbelief as the Berlin Wall come tumbling down. It was the most hopeful, most momentous event of my young life. Now another wall had been built, and I wanted to find out about the lives of the people who lived close to it – on both sides. I began my travels on the Palestinian side.

I had been there only a couple of days when I first came across a shepherd boy. He was sitting alone on a hillside under an olive tree with his sheep grazing all around him. I had seen nothing remotely picturesque in this land until that moment, nothing until now that reminded me in any way of its biblical past. The shepherd boy was making a kite, so intent upon it that he had not noticed my approach. He was whistling softly, not to make a tune, I felt, but simply to reassure his sheep. When he did look up he showed no surprise or alarm. His smile was openhearted and engaging. I could not bring myself to pass by with a mere greeting or a paltry nod of the head.

So I sat down and offered him a drink out of my rucksack. He drank gratefully, eagerly, but said nothing. I patted my camera, told him who I was, shook his hand. I tried to communicate in English, then in the very few words of Arabic I had picked up. His smile was the only reply I got. Clearly he liked me to speak, wanted me to stay, but I knew he didn't understand a word I was saying. So, after a while I lapsed into silence and watched him at work on his kite, the sheep shifting all around us under the shade of the tree, their smell pungent and heavy in the warm air.

When I began to film him he seemed unconcerned, disinterested even. We shared what food we had. He took a great fancy to some Scottish shortbread I'd brought with me from back home in Dundee, and he gave me some of his pine nuts. And we shared our silence too, both of us knowing instinctively that this was fine, as good a way as any to get to know one another.

When evening came and he stood up and began to whistle his sheep home, I knew he expected me to go with him, like one of his sheep. Later, I found myself sitting in his house, surrounded by his huge extended family, all talking amongst each other and watching me, not with hostility, but certainly with some suspicion. It was an unsettling experience. But the boy, I noticed, still said nothing. He was showing everyone the progress he had made with his kite. I could see that he was a much treasured child. We ate lamb, and the most succulent broad beans I had ever tasted, then sweet spiced cake dripping with honey. When the boy came and sat himself down beside me, I knew he was showing me off. I was his guest, and I felt suddenly honoured by that, and moved by his affection.

Then, much to my surprise one of the men spoke to me directly, and in good English. 'I am Said's uncle,' he began. 'You are most welcome in our home. Said would want to say this himself, but he does not speak. Not any more. There was a time when you could not stop him.' He would pause from time to time to explain to everyone what he was telling me. 'It happened two years ago,' he went on. 'Mahmoud was flying his kite on the hill. It was before they built the wall. Mahmoud was Said's elder brother. He loved to make kites. He loved to fly kites. Said was with him. He was always with him. That day, a settler's car had been ambushed down in the valley. Three of them were killed. One was a little girl. Afterwards the soldiers came, and the helicopters. There was some shooting. Maybe it was a revenge killing. Maybe it was a stray bullet. Who knows? Who cares? Mahmoud was shot dead, and Said saw it all. In front of his eyes he saw it. Since this day he does not speak. Since this day he does not grow. God willing he will, God willing. Maybe he is small, maybe he cannot speak, but he is the best shepherd in all Palestine. And you make the best kites too, don't you Said? And Said's kites are not ordinary kites.'

'What do you mean?' I asked.

'Maybe he will show you that himself. Maybe he will fly this kite for you tomorrow. This one is ready to fly, I think. But the wind must always be from the east, or Said will not fly his kites.'

I spent the night under the stars, on the roof of the house. I was tired but far too troubled to sleep. I was up at dawn and went down into the valley. I wanted to film the sun rising over the wall. Once I'd done that, I climbed back up the hill so that I could get a long shot of the wall, tracking it as it sliced obscenely through the olive groves and across the hillside beyond. Dogs barked, and cocks crowed at one another from both sides of the wall.

After breakfast I went off with Said and his sheep, Said carrying his kite, now with its string attached. I doubted he'd be flying it that day because there was very little wind. But an hour or so later, sitting on the highest hill above the village, with the sheep browsing in amongst the rocks, their bells sounding softly, I felt a sudden breeze spring up. Said was on his feet at once, eagerly offering me his kite. I noticed then for the first time that there was writing on one side of the kite, and a drawing too, of a dove.

He was urging me to run now, racing ahead of me to show me how to do it. I felt the wind taking it, felt the kite suddenly air-borne, wind-whipped and tugging to be free. Said clapped his hands in wild delight as it swooped and soared above us. I had done this on Hampstead Heath with my father when I was a boy, but had forgotten the sheer exhilaration of it. The kite was alive at the end of the string, loving it as much as I was. Said tapped my arm and took the string from me. Very reluctantly, I handed it over.

Said was an expert. With a tweak of his wrist the kite turned and twirled, with a flick of his fingers he dived it and danced it. My professional instinct kicked in. I needed boy and kite in the same shot, so I had to put some distance between them and me. I backed away over the hillside, pausing to film as I went, fearful of missing these fleeting moments of innocent rapture in this war-ravaged land. I closed on the fluttering kite, then zoomed in on the wall below, following it up over the hillside, and focussing on the settlement beyond, on the flag flying there, and then on some children playing football in the street below. I watched them through my lens, witnessed the celebratory hugging as one of them scored.

I turned my camera on Said again. There was, I noticed, a look of intense concentration on his face. That was the moment he let the kite go. It was quite deliberate. He simply gave it to the wind, holding his arms aloft as if he'd just released a trapped bird, and was giving it its freedom. It soared up high, seeming to float there for a while on the thermals, before the wind discovered it and took it away over the olive grove, over the wall and up towards the hill-top settlement.

Said was tugging at my arm again. He wanted to look through my lens. I saw then what he was looking at; a young girl in a headscarf gazing up at the kite as it came floating down. Now she was running over to where it had landed. She picked it up and stood looking at us for a few moments, before the footballers came racing down the hill towards her. They all stood there then, gazing across at us. But when Said waved, only the girl in the headscarf waved back. They didn't fly the kite. They just took it away and disappeared.

On the way home with the sheep later that day, we came across Said's uncle harvesting his broad beans. 'It's a poor crop, but what can you do?' he said. 'There is never enough water. They take all our best land, all our water. They leave us only the dust to farm in.' I stayed to talk while Said walked on up into the village with his sheep. 'So the wind was right,' Said's uncle went on. 'Said never keeps his kites you know, not one. He just makes them, waits for the east wind, and sends them off. Did you see what he draws on each one? A dove of peace. Did you see what he writes? Salaam. Shalom. And he signs every one of them: Mahmoud and Said.'

'How many has he sent?' I asked.

'A hundred maybe. About one a week since they killed Mahmoud. He wrote it down for his mother once, telling her why he does it. For Said, every kite that lands over there is like a seed of friendship. He believes that one day they'll send the kites back, and everything will be right, friendships will grow, and peace will come and the killing will stop. Let him have his dreams. It's all he has. He'll find out soon enough what they're like over there.'

'There was a girl who found the kite,' I told him. 'She waved back. I saw her. It's a beginning.'

'It costs nothing to wave,' he replied bitterly.

I stayed one more night. So I was there to see the embryo of the next kite taking shape, Said kneeling on the carpet, his whole family watching intently as he constructed the frame with infinite care, ignoring all their advice, and the food and drink they constantly offered him. 'Maybe it is good,' Said's uncle said to me, when Said had gone up to bed, 'Maybe it helps him to forget. Maybe if he forgets, he will find his voice again. Maybe he will grow again. God willing. God willing.'

I said my goodbyes early the next morning and left with Said and the sheep. Said held my hand all the way. There was between us, I felt, the same unspoken thought: that we were friends and did not want to part, and that when we did we would probably never see each other again. The sheep were in clambering mood, their bells jangling loud in the morning air. We sat down on the hillside where we'd flown the kite the day before. Said had brought the frame of his new kite with him, but he was not in the mood for working on it. Like me he was gazing out over the valley, over the wall, towards the settlement. The flag still fluttered there. A donkey brayed balefully nearby, winding itself up into a frenzy of misery. I felt it was time for me to go. I put my hand on Said's shoulder, let it rest there a few moments, then left him.

When I looked back a while later, he was busy with his kite. I stopped to film him. It would be the perfect closing shot. I had just about got myself ready to film when Said sprang to his feet. The sheep were suddenly bounding away from him, scattering across the hillside.

47

Then I saw the kites. They were all colours of the rainbow, hundreds of them, like dancing butterflies they were, rising into the air from the hillside below the settlement. I could hear the shrieks of joy, saw the crowd of children gathered there, everyone of them flying a kite. A few snagged each other and plunged to earth, but most sailed up triumphantly heavenwards. The settlers were pouring out of their houses to watch. One after the other, the kites were released, took wind and flew out over the wall towards us. And from behind me, from Said's village, the people came running, as the kites landed in amongst us, and amongst the terrified sheep too. On every kite I saw the same message, in English and in Hebrew: 'Shalom and Salaam'. And on every kite too there was a drawing of an olive branch. Everywhere on both sides of the wall the children were cheering and laughing and dancing about. I could see the girl in the scarf waving at us, and leaping up and down.

Around me, some of the mothers and fathers, grandmothers and grandfathers, began to clap too, hesitantly at first. But others soon joined in, Said's uncle amongst them. But the cheering, I noticed, and the laughter and the dancing they left to the children. The hillsides rang with their jubilation, with their exultation. It seemed to me like a symphony of hope.

As I raced over the hillside towards Said, I could hear him laughing and shouting out loud along with all the others. I realised then - idiot that I was - that I had quite forgotten to film this miracle. And almost simultaneously I understood that it didn't matter anyway, that it was the laughter that mattered. It was laughter that would one day resonate so loud that this wall would come tumbling down. No trumpets needed, as they had been at Jericho, only the laughter of children.

Mrs Eastcott

Jane Feaver

It was odd he hadn't come down. Not like him. But it was a Sunday: natural enough to take advantage of that fact. And perhaps he'd had a busy day yesterday - he'd been out until supper time. She'd leave it a bit.

When Mr and Mrs Whitehead had paid up, it was just him and her. She couldn't help thinking that it felt nice, him upstairs. He was cleaner than she'd ever known a man; he smelt of coal-tar soap. It was something she noticed: how people brought their own smell into the house. She took care to replace the air-freshener in the lounge and in the upstairs bathroom: it was the price paid for having strangers in. Worst were the couples in the double room, the smell of wrestling, of unfinished business. And it was distasteful, the way they'd leave a bed, unmade, shaken up. Sometimes, she put on rubber gloves to change the sheets and averted her eyes in case she saw a mess. She liked those couples best who expressly chose the twin.

After his first visit, she always put Mr Webber in her favourite room, the small double overlooking the square. The room reminded her of her mother, not surprising in that it contained the residue of furniture her mother had left her: the mahogany chest of drawers with the silver swan handles, the pin-striped nursing chair, a pink and green vanity set and her eiderdown with its May-queen celebration of flowers. She'd chosen honeysuckle wallpaper and painted the window seat in white gloss, plumped a lacy cushion in one corner. It was peaceful in there.

Sometimes, when she was empty of guests, she'd open the window and perch on the edge of the bed. The room was high up and it didn't take much of a breeze for the air to rush in, sluicing down the angular walls and ceiling, nudging at the inverted light shade. *Do the dusting for me*, she'd think. On days when she woke up too early, she'd wrap herself in her dressing gown, go into the lighter room and sit listening for the clink of the milk float, making herself feel tearful by the easy way it managed to get going - humming, always positive. Or on dark evenings in winter, when the square would be tinny with rain, she'd spy on the boys who gathered round the lamp by the old pump, shoving each other with cans of lager.

In the kitchen the clock ticked like a pulse, half past nine. This morning she was making an effort to avoid looking up at it. Like the time she'd spent with Brian on the ward, waiting for the nervous bleep of the machine.

Ten years was a long time to be on your own.

With other guests, the waiting would have been an irritation, a hindrance to getting on. With Mr Webber it was something else: anticipation, perhaps. She looked forward to their morning chats. But 'look forward' was too restrained. It had become more than that; like the first cup of the day, she thirsted for it.

On Monday he was leaving and she didn't want to waste a minute. Love at first sight, well that was silly. She wasn't saying that. It was just that there was something about the way his face, over all others she had ever known, responded to hers; its peculiar mobility and the way he absorbed what she would say and return it to her, wrapped up somehow, as if he took notice.

Morning. There was a note he'd hit at the base of his voice that stirred the core of her. And then his head would appear around the door, questioning, before emerging full body in his mustard coloured waistcoat, pulling at his cuffs, twiddling the mother-of-pearl cuff-links, the gleaming conkers of his shoes.

She knew his routine. He had two bristle brushes which he kept upturned on the chest of drawers, and he would have shaved already so that his skin would be shining, when he came down, like a blue hydrangea. He took nothing for granted, standing until she said, 'Have a chair,' and he'd bow slightly and go and sit in the table by the window where she'd have lain a copy of the *Western Morning News.*

If he'd been up with her late at night, the mornings were a strange realignment of formalities. Last night, for instance, he'd told her his first name: Eustace. Not a name, although she tried, that she could bring herself to say. It was a posh name. From a different class. And yet he always treated her with the utmost respect. 'Very well, thank you, Mrs Eastcott, slept like a log,' he'd say, not at all as if he were out of her grasp.

It was unusual to have a man like that on his own, someone who had no purpose - no brewery inspection, no ruby anniversary - but to be there. And one who appreciated her little touches; the bowls of pot pourri and scented wood chips in the bathroom. This was his third Easter in a row and she'd got to know a bit about him. She was happy, after dinner, to let him sit up with her, in Brian's chair. She'd buy in bottled beer or cider, and then, if they were still full of talk, she'd dig out the sherry or the port.

You wouldn't have believed a profession like that still existed, not in this day and age, but that's what he was, after the army: a butler, he called it, up country, one of those huge stately homes, for the Duke of Somewhere. And he had been married, once, though his wife had been much younger and it hadn't lasted. Played tennis. Ran off with a man from the tennis club. He told her how for a while, he'd gone off the rails and they'd stopped him driving, got in a chauffeur. Kept him on though, let him have a suite of rooms in one of the wings. He was the only one allowed in the morning into the Duke's bedroom to give him his pills; saw the state of him some days: excrement - though he wasn't that specific - in the sheets. Twenty seven years of service he'd given by the time they let him go.

Little things she noticed about him. Like no dandruff on his collar, the paper-sharp press of his creases. It's not that Brian hadn't kept himself clean, but he was more slap-dash than meticulous. He'd never been quite the same after the plate was put in, a big dent in his forehead like an old enamel jug.

She was always straightening him up, wiping egg from his beard before they left the house.

Perhaps it was the difference that took her unawares. Mr Webber was like a man in a book, the man when she was a little girl, who would have been going off to work with a hat in a black shiny car to an office. Brian was more her own kind. They'd been at school together, muddled along, him part-time in *Cornwall Farmers*, good around the house. He played cricket in the summer for the pub and, like her father, had been a stalwart of the band. A euphonium player. He had the perfect build for it: short legs, a barrel of a chest.

It was only after the operation when Brian played sometimes that she worried about his head. Though the doctors said it would be fine, it made her anxious to watch him go forever without pausing for breath. She wasn't musical; all she could hear was the high-pitched shrill of a kettle that wouldn't let off until it burnt dry. He prided himself like a deep sea diver, and she'd be listening to him, holding on in sympathy, feeling herself drowning before he ever thought of surfacing for air.

They were like brother and sister. She found herself, even this long after, saying his name under her breath like a prayer. It wasn't like in books or at the pictures: not the passion, the slow undressing. He was too much the same as she was.

When Mr Webber came for the second time, the shock of recognition, of seeing his features fall like a mirror into place, took her unexpectedly. She wanted everything to be right for him; annoyed by guests who came back late and would disturb him, or the young couple down for a wedding who made animal noises all night.

This year, he'd booked six months ahead. She found herself looking forward to 7th April, drawing a flower head around the date in her calendar, and writing neatly *Mr Webber* with an arrow over the next page and writing it again on the Monday, *Mr Webber goes*.

Once she had Christmas out of the way, the ditchwater of January, February and March, she began to pick up and the weeks, busier now, slipped into each other in a round of cleaning and putting out the bins. She'd learnt a lot about the human race doing this. Too much, sometimes, she thought. The way people would leave a room for her to tidy in the day - stinking socks, underwear, body sprays, nests of knotted hair, splashes of nail varnish - as if she were a skivvy; sometimes it drove her to despair. Her home, part of her. How cross Brian would have been to see her treated like that. How humiliating if Mr Webber could have known.

There were certain things she missed about being married: the way people didn't fidget after you, but left you to get on; those quiet intimacies of morning tea, a nip of something before bed. And the worst thing, the balance of a room when someone else was there: the lack of balance when they'd gone.

The Bed and Breakfast idea had been something they'd discussed together years before Brian died. It would be a way of managing to keep the house, when really it was too big for the two of them, into their retirement. They'd not had children and although once or twice over the years of their marriage they'd broached the question of adoption, or fostering even, to test the water, they'd never had the gumption to push it through - all the form-filling, the assessments, the waiting. And what if it turned out wrong? Stories you heard, when the child like a cuckoo turned you out of your own home.

When Brian died it became a project. With some of the insurance money she got Mr Fawcett in to sort the arrangements, surprised at how easy it was to realise her specifications, putting extra pink sinks in the bedrooms, hooks on the doors for coats, papering, a lick of paint. It would be done as if by magic, handing over the cash to him at the end of the week in an envelope of neatly counted notes.

Nine-fifty. Nine-fifty-one. She could feel herself agitating. What if he got up and had to rush straight off? She had envisaged time to make further purchase. There was something he'd said last night about the place had lit her up, that *here would be as good as anywhere*. She wanted to breathe life on those embers.

It wasn't that she didn't think of Brian. Quite the reverse. If she'd have asked him, she was sure he'd have approved of her extra touches, her gracious accommodation of strangers. She'd have negotiated past him, bumbling about the kitchen in his slippers, to reach down, as she did now, for the pony tray, its little wicker fence to keep the things in place. She liked to use the heather-sprig china for best, and took a cup from the sideboard, the matching jug and sugar bowl, gave them a shine with the drying-up cloth. Laying the linen napkin with its four-leafed clovers, its flying orange geese, was something her mother would have done. And she'd bought a box of sugar cubes for the miniature-clawed silver tongs they'd had as a wedding present. She swilled the pot.

While she waited for the tea to brew she sat down with her hand laid over her belly to settle her stomach. Her handbag was on the fridge and she reached over for it, defiantly took out a coral lipstick and, without looking in the mirror, smoothed its tip along the upper outline of her mouth, then pressed her lips together like a butterfly, rolling the colour in. She fluffed her hair around her ears, lifted the apron over her head like leather tack.

Casting a final eye over the tray, she adjusted the cloth and then she grasped it to her, arms full width, feeling the muscles and the bones as if she were working a contraption separate from herself, and backed through the narrow door into the pit of the steep stairway.

If you stood at the bottom, it was like watching someone climb a chimney. She took each tread blindly, raising a leg as if she were under water. As she did so, she imagined him turning in surprise - pleasant surprise - his striped pyjamas open at the neck, her sitting gently on the edge of his bed.

She had crept up earlier, pretending to herself that she was checking the adjacent room - the man-trap of a floorboard that groaned as she passed - and had listened for a moment at his door. Not a flicker. This time she made no effort to disguise her ascent and stood determinedly in the same spot, heard herself calling cheerfully, 'Morning!'

There was no response. She cleared her throat and adjusted the tray on to the bracket of her knee, knocked hastily to keep her balance, 'Morning, Mr Webber!'

Still no answer. She felt a pang of foolishness, crossness with him for making her look a fool. It was too late to retreat. She pressed on, taking the bulbous handle of the door and turning it, grabbed the tray almost simultaneously and nudged into the room, 'Morn-....'

The word reared in her mouth and the tray rocked forward, sliding crockery to its wicker edge. And then, as if in slow motion, the milk came toppling over, flung to the pink carpet, snow melting into the pile. The cup broke clean in two, its saucer rolling under the bed, and then the tea-pot lid - hats off - tea-leaves spattering like ants in a steamy jungle.

Her arms dropped like chains; the tray hit the floor. She turned away into the corridor, aghast, eyes greedily taking in the paper border of Egyptian hieroglyphs, the gilt frames of a pair of Constable's, the light switch. But every detail she strove to fix lurched at her now as if they were on a sinking ship. The frame of the door behind her was breathing down her neck as if it were a person.

'Mr Webber?' she said in the corridor like a child locked in a dark cupboard.

She gulped, clenched her teeth and forced herself to turn round. Slowly she put her hand up to her mouth, bit a finger.

The eiderdown was turned over. The man she saw, who'd been so spruce, so well turned out, now lay - it made her think of a pig, of a pantomime - flat out on the bed. He was wearing a red cotton dress, open at the side, its zip gaping, and his pink flesh showing through like raw chicken. The short-sleeves were stretched at the seams with little hyphens of stitches over the tops of his arms, whose skin expanded like sausage skin, pale and freckled. One arm, a cantilever, out from the bed. His legs were dead straight and hairless, goose-fleshed. There were maroon socks on his feet, and elastic braces for holding them up. Drunk? Asleep? But she knew not, by the yellow-grey pallor of his skin.

'Brian' she whispered, when she meant to say 'God'. The name Eustace too sprung to mind, and the thought, suddenly, that maybe, after all, it might be a woman's name.

Then she heard a tinkling sound, the sink in the corner, gurgling, lifting a weight of scum and suds, about to brim over. She hurried across the room with half an eye out for the body as if it might yet spring up from the bed, and turned off the idling tap. She could see the water wasn't draining properly, something was blocking it, not the iron filings of a chin, but finer, longer hair, like weed in a pond

There was a sweaty puddle of dark carpet around the pedestal. The drip continued like a clock. She stood facing the bed. His skin was waxy, overblown magnolia and his hair was vigorous, fox-like. She swallowed. The burden of what she would have to do felt as if it would bring the ceiling crashing down on her. Doctor. Police. She moved in tiny steps towards the bedside. A red dress with flowers of blue and green. It was something her mother might have worn, something from the War.

'Mr Webber?' she said, still hoping that it was a terrible, unfortunate joke and that he would come round and come clean. She put a hand out to the fabric where it touched his knee, swallowing again. Perhaps she should take the dress off? She drew the hem a little upward, looking at his face, his blear marble eyes, rolled to the roof of their sockets, and could see where his tongue had pressed forward, bluish with a bubble of spittle where it met the serrated edge of his teeth. The dress would lift as far as the waist and no further: no way of getting it off but by embracing him, lifting him upright in a semi-dance. She shivered.

But she was curious. Who would be looking now if she looked? There was a boy at school, Tom Brookes, who got taken away in the end because he wouldn't stop showing the girls. It was like a little slug or a snail, that's all she remembered, and the way they used to run to the teacher, 'Miss, Miss - he done it again!' covering their mouths like their mothers did, as if they were going to be sick.

And Brian, he did it without a word to her, not roughly or anything, but as if, *we'll do it and then we'll draw a veil*, as though it never happened. She let him turn from her and tuck himself away. Once or twice she spotted him in the bath, but he'd always rise up, like Neptune, with the cloudy water around him and a tidal wave against the taps, covering himself with his hands.

She lifted the hem as if there was something still living in there, a snake or a creature that would jump up. She peeped. Mr Webber's legs were straight out and between them, in a warm, soft nest of tawny hair, there was a little bald mouse curled up. It was so beside itself that, when all the others had fled, it had shut its eyes tight against the great clapping machine as if, keeping dead still, everything would go away, dreaming of how things might have been, like a soldier, a lion.

A Clean Life in the North

Jean Rafferty

We crouched in the long grass, waiting. You can see cars approaching from miles away, then they dip out of sight before re-appearing on the long, curved road up to our farm. It was hot, even this late in the afternoon, and my head hurt. Susannnah popped a piece of black seaweed blown up from the beach below. It was shaped like a cockroach but no slime oozed from it when she cracked it. 'What a pity. It wasn't alive,' she said, her laugh weird, unnatural. 'We could have offered it to the Dark Goddess.'

'Shut up.' I couldn't stand hearing her talk about that stuff. She was always hyper for days, sometimes weeks afterwards, her eyes too bright, her voice too loud. I concentrated on breathing in the smell of the rough, salty grass. Susannah wouldn't keep still. She was wriggling about, searching for bugs in the ground. 'For God's sake, stop that,' I said. I felt as if the sun was suffocating me.

'I hate Sister Mary Anthony. Stupid name anyway. How dare she come poking her nose in?'

Susannah hates religion, her and my mother both. Strange, when they both have Biblical names. Mother's Bathsheba, after the mother of Solomon, which is a joke. She'll never be wise if she lives to 100 years old. Susannah is after the woman taken in adultery, but Mother's so blinkered against good things that she doesn't know the real story - Susannah was innocent and proved that the men who accused her were just leches themselves.

I don't like any religions, but I love Sister Mary Anthony. She was the first teacher to notice something was wrong in our family, though even now she doesn't know the half of it. She's young and gentle, not like some of the crabby nuns. My brother Flynn says those old bags could do with a good fuck, though I don't see why they'd want to. Too sore.

I saw Sister Mary Anthony when the school rabbit was killed. She was crying, holding the poor wee beast in her arms, its head dangling down. 'Who would do this to an innocent creature?' she asked. I shrugged, though it wasn't hard for me to think of possible rabbit assassins. Killing such a small animal was nothing to my brothers.

'Will you help me bury it? I don't think anyone but us needs to know, do you? Some of the younger children would be dreadfully upset.'

I said yes, amazed that she would trust one of the wild Mackies. People think we're out of control; nobody realises how much we keep secret. We have to, Mother says, or else the Goddess and her three sons will abandon us and we'll become powerless like the idiots around us. Now that I'm 15 I don't think other people look so idiotic, but Susannah loves the idea of the sons - Darkness, Violence and Evil they're called. They have other names, daft Celtic ones - Dub, Dian and Dother. She says she's seen them in the clearing, conjuring themselves up out of the fire when we chant. 'They're really handsome,' she says. '*Built*. You know what I mean?' Like I care.

The goddess Carman and her three sons are the reason we came north. Not that I knew about them then. We were living in a farm down south, raising horses. We made a lot of money from them. They were beautiful, though I didn't like seeing how they suffered. Father tied them to a tractor and ran them along the beach for training. Lots of racehorse people do, but he always lashed their heads too tightly. They were so fine and graceful, even when tethered to the stubby machine. I hated it that they weren't able to run free. I let them go from the stable once, but Father made sure I didn't dare go near them again for months.

When Mother said we were coming north I was ecstatic. I was too little to know. I dreamed of a land far away, a land of ice and snow, of high mountains and pure, clean water. I'd seen that stupid film and I thought Scotland was full of brave people in kilts and blue face paint who'd stop the bad things happening, but it was just like home. Nobody wanted to believe that people were so cruel.

We travelled north in a big jeep carrying a caravan behind us. They often use that caravan for the dirty stuff they do. There's a trap door in it and they shove you down there or lock you in the toilet if anyone comes. Sometimes they do that just to scare us. 'The spiders that live down the bog watch everything you do,' Mother says. 'They've got a big network of relatives all over the country, so don't ever think you can get away with anything. They tell us everything.' I know now that spiders are too caught up in their dumb webs to bother about humans, but I'm still scared of them.

The journey north was tedious. Susannah and I were in the caravan with Flynn and one of our other brothers, Jack. They spent the whole time being annoying. They flicked pellets at us, tickled us, made farting noises and pretended it was us. Susannah acted as if she was annoyed, but she wasn't really. She loved Flynn too much. She ended up snuggled on the bed with him, letting him put his hand up her skirt whenever he wanted. The caravan rocked and swayed all the way north and made me feel sick. We should never have been in it while it was moving but Mother and Father didn't care about stuff like that.

The journey took a day and a half. They let us out when we crossed over on the ferry. It was wonderful, seeing the rough waves and smelling the salt green water. I thought it would be a new beginning, a *clean* life. We rolled off the ferry and drove for miles, up the long road and through the hills, till there ahead of us was this farmhouse, even more isolated than the last one we lived in. They parked the caravan right by the side door. That was when I knew that we may have come north but we had brought our own world with us. I knew then there would be no escape.

That night we all sat round the big round table we'd brought from the south. Mother lit candles. 'May God not be with us and the light not be upon us,' she said, passing her hand through the flame. There was a lot of stuff about the Great Dark Goddess who had brought us to this place, but I tried to block that rubbish out. I just thought about being on the boat and seeing a new life waiting for us. When that didn't work I went further back and pretended that we hadn't got here at all, that the north still lay ahead.

Now, lying in the long grass with Susannah, I wondered if I would ever have the courage to run away, even when I was older. I didn't want to be like the others. I didn't feel the power they felt. I hated it. Sometimes I hated them. I looked at Susannah and the malicious smile on her face and I dreaded what was to come. There was a meanness about her, hugging her plans to her like a shrivelled old walnut. Some Goddess. More like fucking Rumpelstiltskin.

I wished I could warn Sister Mary Anthony, but I didn't know what to tell her. *My sister the psychopath is out to get you.* That day of the rabbit murder Sister wiped away her tears and said, 'Come on, sweetheart.' To *me*. Of course I followed her like a daft little dog. We went to the janitor's shed and she got a couple of spades out. 'I know a good place to bury it, Sister,' I said. I took her beyond the school and down into the woods. I steered her away from the path till I found the clearing where we did the chanting. Even though no-one was here I felt cold. I knew what would happen to me if any of them found out I'd brought a nun to this place. But I wanted her to *see*.

She didn't, of course. I was going to start digging where we always buried the animals they gave to the goddess, but Sister Mary Anthony had already started near the place of the altar. 'This is funny. Looks like someone's camped here overnight. There's been a fire here.' She frowned. 'I don't like this place, do you?'

I looked round. The trees around us were moving in the wind. It was as if I could see evil spirits flitting through the branches, hear the screams of creatures being sacrificed. Every bush held the fear-frozen face of a child, every churned-up piece of mud the imprint of feet trying to flee.

'You look dreadful, Emerald. Are you all right?' Her face was kind. She looked like she really cared about me. I gradually stopped shivering and saw that the trees were still trees, the mud only mud. We started digging and it felt like we were making something good here, where before had been only bad. Sister Mary Anthony began singing that poxy song from 'The Sound of Music,' *The hills are alive...* I could hardly stop laughing, it seemed so ludicrous after what I'd been thinking. Sister smiled her sunny smile and said, 'I'm glad you're back to yourself, dear.'

We dug for ages. It was heavy work and I could hear the Sister breathing hard beside me. For the first time ever I felt like part of a team, instead of one powerless little person lost among madmen. When the hole was deep enough Sister Mary Anthony said, 'We need a shroud.' She slipped her hand under her skirt and pulled down a white waist slip. She wasn't embarrassed as I'd have been or flirtatious like Susannah, just really solemn. She knelt on the ground and spread the underskirt out. Then she laid the rabbit down on the white cotton, as gently as if it were still alive, and wrapped the little creature up. It was only a rabbit but I felt I could die of sadness.

Sister Mary Anthony made the sign of the cross, then whispered the words of some prayer. It sounded beautiful. I looked round this place I hated and it was as if it had become fresh and green again, as if it had drawn nourishment from her kindness. I think places can do that, hold the spirit of the people who've used them. I hoped hers was stronger than theirs.

Carefully she started dropping spadefuls of soil on top of the body. The white fabric became dusty and dark and was finally obliterated. We tamped down the soil as best we could, then Sister pulled some broken branches over it. 'Rest in peace,' she said to the little animal under the ground.

She took me into the convent on the way home and made me some hot chocolate. There was a picture of the Sacred Heart on the wall and I stared at it for ages, willing myself to believe in Jesus for her sake. I couldn't. So he had suffered for other people's sins? There were plenty of people in the world like that. Sister must know he wasn't the only one.

Now I was crouched in the grass, waiting for something awful to happen. Dusk was falling when we saw the nuns' car in the hills. I panicked and went to get up, but Susannah twisted my wrist and forced me back down. She's much bigger and stronger than me. 'Mother'll love this,' she said. 'Fuck the nuns.'

She got up and pulled me into the middle of the road. 'Take your knickers down,' she said. I could feel my face going bright red. 'Don't be stupid,' I said. She yanked at them, but I was so desperate I twisted out of her grasp. I ran hell for leather towards the rocks. The car's headlights bored up the road, made the familiar dip. I grazed the whole front of my leg, scrambling up the rocks in the dark. Susannah crouched down in the road, her skirt hoicked up. The nuns' car swept into sight again, the bright yellow lights picking out Susannah's pale arse, the blue string of the tampon she yanked out of herself, the thick gunk of brown on the road. The car slowed to a complete halt and I could see Sister Mary Anthony's shocked face. I couldn't move. Susannah was laughing her stupid head off. 'Fuck off back where you came from,' she shouted.

It seemed like minutes before Sister Mary Anthony started the engine up again. She didn't say a word, just started to turn the car round. The headlights swung across the rocks where I was standing. Sister Mary Anthony stared straight at me as if I was someone she didn't know. As she drove away, Susannah chucked her tampon at the back window, sending a streak of black blood down the glass. 'You bloody wanker,' she said. 'Too fucking scared, were you? Nuns shit just like the rest of us, you know.'

I started running after the car then, but it had already gone down into the dip. 'Wait for me,' I shouted, but the engine was making too much noise and the wind tore my words away. I wanted to keep running and running but I had nowhere to go. Slowly I turned back up the hill towards Susannah. I was crying, not really thinking where I was going. I stepped right in the pile of shit. She was laughing so hard, she was wheezing. 'Serves you right,' she said.

I yanked a lump of grass from the side of the road and started scrubbing at my shoe. I wondered how Sister Mary Anthony could believe in anything. There was a design flaw in the idea of God. It's not that he lets all the cruelty in the world go on or that he's abandoned the black people and lets them starve while the white ones get fatter and fatter. It's not the sodding ugly unfairness of it all. It's the shit.

My hand slipped and the stuff came right through the grass on to my skin. I was retching at the putrid stink of it. I thought, what God in his right mind would make people carry such a disgusting substance around inside themselves? And I knew that no matter how far north I went I would never get myself clean.

Sans Everything

Nel Boswood

Harold drives to the hospital in the morning rain. It is still dark and will be for another hour, for this is the dead of winter. At first he takes the country lanes just outside the London Orbital. There are no signs of life; even the trees look as if they have been painted or embossed onto the illuminated orange sky. It is silent in the car, which he prefers for concentration.

Once within the ring of the M25 the scene quickly becomes urban and to his surprise the roads here are already clogged and busy. He has run into the beginning of what the weathermen now call the morning rush, something he hasn't encountered for years, not since his retirement. It has changed: there is an aggressive self-importance and lack of courtesy in the way these drivers behave. They seem to have no shame.

Harold takes his time, remains courteous, lets people from side-streets into the space in front of him, only to infuriate the drivers behind who beep angrily. This makes him stubborn and even more deliberate in his politeness. At least he knows the route now, so he won't be dithering at the busier junctions. He came yesterday to bring Gail in for her operation, and before that there were the outpatient appointments, and then not so long ago the scare with the lump in her breast when they had to come several times.

The hospital is sprawling, seeming to have grown in an unplanned way with the new portacabin-style additions to the original red-brick Victorian construction. Gail is in an old ward, two flights up – he remembers the route from yesterday, but it still feels like a maze. His nostrils fill with the stink of disinfectant in the warm gloom as his feet scuff on the non-slip grey floor.

He is nervous as he walks into the ward and tries to detect Gail's mood before she sees him. This will permit him to compose himself into the person she needs him to be. Getting it right tends to save awkwardness, something that has become more important recently. Today he spots her before she does him. She is straining her body forward, trying to sit up and not quite managing.

She's trying to get the attention of the nurse nearest to her, which he sees is impossible as there is one patient shouting 'Help!' extremely loudly about three beds down from her and another opposite who has vomited. The nurse is hesitating over which patient to attend to first, momentarily paralysed by indecision, but definitely not looking at Gail.

He smiles, walks haltingly over to Gail and helps her to sit up.

'How are you my love?'

'Thank God you're here. I need a wash and no-one's taking any notice of me.' The irritation spits from her. He relaxes. This is familiar, this is comfortable. He can deal with it.

'How was the night?' he asks, but she is not looking at him. She is looking fiercely at another nurse who has just emerged from behind a curtain.

'Please – I need a wash', she says loudly. 'I've been waiting at least half an hour.'

The nurse gives Gail a look of exasperation, though her voice remains calm. 'We're short-staffed so it's taking longer than usual. We'll be with you in a minute.'

'Perhaps if you brought me some water, I could do it', says Harold helpfully. The nurse looks no less irritated but does bring a bowl of warm water and some soap, which she leaves on the table at the foot of the bed. Harold, with some difficulty, begins to close the curtains around the bed and as he does so is unable to avoid looking at the gaunt yellow face of the woman in the bed to Gail's right. She is uncomfortably near. He is glad that her eyes are closed so he does not have to attempt a greeting. On the other side a tiny shrivelled-looking woman is hunched on her side on top of her bed covers with her back to them. The thinness of her body is not hidden by the light garment she is wearing. He buries his panic, looking instead at Gail as he tugs and coaxes the snagging curtains. She is flushed, perspiring, and her hair is wild. She certainly does not look as ill as the people around her. He feels proud of her strength and resilience, grateful.

'I can wash myself. Just take my nightie off, could you?' she says once they are cocooned within their own private space. He wheels the table with the water on it up to her end of the bed and helps her lift first one buttock, then the other, easing the nightdress upwards. She feels solid to him, but smells unfamiliar. He edges the nightdress gently over her upper torso and head, noticing how white her body is in contrast with the high colour of her face and neck. There is a dressing over the area of her belly button which looks damp, a dark orange stain in the middle of it. He does not mention this for fear of irritating her further and sparking another outburst at the nurse.

Harold finds Gail's flannel in the bedside locker and hands it to her. She soaps and rinses her face, hairline and neck with obvious relief and manages a quick dab under her arms, under her breasts and between the tops of her thighs.

'Could you do my feet?' she commands rather than asks, and he obliges, relieved to have something to do other than watch. First he has to remove the white pressure socks which are squeezing her calves tightly. They leave an angry red line just above her knees. He takes the soap, dips it into the water and turns it in his hands. He reaches for his wife's right foot. She relaxes back on the pillow and an unexpected pleasure steals over him as he takes the foot in his hands and begins to massage it. He can't ever remember having done this for her before, in spite of their many years of shared intimacy. He has tickled her feet, yes, or grabbed one while cavorting on the beach, or stroked one furtively with his own foot under the table at a dinner party, but washed? Why hadn't he? He finds himself thinking of the little time left to them and the enormous quantity of things not yet done, pleasures not taken, chances and opportunities not used and now beyond reach.

His thoughts return to an image that, unusually, remains from a dream he had last night. The image is of his old army rucksack, the one that he still uses despite its fraying, clumsily patched canvas, the golden brown colour of which has faded to pale porridge. He may not have recalled this image at all were it not for the fact that he had found Polly, one of their terriers, asleep on it on the kitchen floor this morning. This had jolted the picture from his subconscious, along with a feeling, which was one of sadness.

He finds Gail's foot solid and strong. He can feel her indignation and resilience pulsing through it. It calms him. He continues soaping, does not want to stop. When he begins on the other one, he lingers and delays, paying careful attention to the tender places between the toes, and gently pressing certain points on her wide soles. He feels tears coming to his eyes and looks at the sheet until the feeling goes away. She is looking at him with an open, vacant stare.

A nurse bursts through the curtains – 'Oh,' she says without surprise or apology. 'We'd better cover you up – the consultant's coming.'

Gail's earlier irritation has disappeared, and she willingly dons clean nightwear and settles on the bed. 'That feels better,' she says and closes her eyes. The consultant does not in fact arrive for another 25 minutes, so they wait in a silence punctuated by the regular and harsh cries for help from the woman three beds down.

'What's wrong with her?' asks Harold. 'Can't they do something?'

'No – they're going to put her in a different ward in a little while.'

Gail seems immune to the distress in the calls and the nurses don't respond to them either. They carry on with their routine duties, looking harried and exhausted. Harold wonders if they are at the end of a long shift, or if they have just started. It is impossible to tell. There is a brusqueness in their movements and their facial expressions, not, he realises, from any bad feeling towards their patients, but from an instinct for self-preservation, from a need to conserve energy, not to be brought down.

The consultant arrives looking like someone from a bank or a city business. He has an entourage of white-coated young people, none of whom are introduced to Harold or Gail. While the consultant checks Gail's paperwork and then her wound these young people look on as if at a biological specimen in a lab, a couple of them shuffling nervously. Harold finds himself pondering courtesy again, but is too tired to follow any logical line of thought and succumbs to a feeling of resignation.

A few cursory comments and the consultant, plus entourage, have gone, leaving one of the nurses to dress the wound. It seems the biopsy results will be ready later today and that Gail must stay in another night. When they get the results they will know what action to take next, action being the euphemism for chemo, radio or whatever new therapy they decide to employ. If, as he hardly dares hope, the tumour in her gut turns out to be benign, presumably no action will be needed, and they will return home thankful for another reprieve, a further postponement of the inevitable, but unthinkable.

They don't talk about this, although they have, of course, at home, in private. Instead, Gail tells him about the annoying man a few beds down who has a radio, and how she had to ask the nurses to make him turn it down. He tells her about the traffic this morning, how the dogs are missing her, and who has phoned with good wishes. He wants to tell her how much he liked washing her feet, imagining the smile this might raise, but it feels inappropriate amid the flat, insipid despair of the ward.

After a while Gail dozes. Harold looks at the dog-eared sheet of paper in the plastic folder above the head of her bed and the hand-written message on it: 'Nil by mouth'. The sign is lop-sided, hastily scrawled and looks like instructions for a punishment. His attention drifts to the whitening sky that he can see through the high sash-windows and further fragments of his dream start to come back to him. Slowly, he pieces together a scene in which he is about to take a long sea-voyage. His packed rucksack is ready waiting on the ship, as it should be. After all, this rucksack has been everywhere with him. He can't remember a time when he didn't have it. Aware that there is more in the dream and that it is significant, he strains to recapture it.

Another scene arrives all in a rush from some hidden place in his mind, and it stabs at his heart. He is standing alone on the shore watching the ship steaming towards the horizon without him. He realises it is carrying his rucksack away.

Gail has woken and is in pain. Her face is grey. 'Love, do you want me to get a nurse?' he whispers. She nods. In spite of the earlier bustle on the ward, there are now no nurses in sight. He finds one in an office near the door, who comes at once.

'Yes – it's time for a top-up,' she agrees, and goes away, returning with a syringe.

'Is it the same dose I had last time?' asks Gail, quite agitated now.

'Yes'

'Can you up it? It's not touching the pain,' says Gail.

'I will if you're still bad in half an hour' says the nurse firmly.

For what seems a long time Gail grimaces in silence. Her legs twitch and her fingers grope the stiff sheet. Her chest heaves irregularly, but the sound of her breathing becomes imperceptible, as if her body has focussed its energy elsewhere than on the mundane task of drawing air. Gradually, she is calmer. She lies with her eyes open, an empty, exhausted look on her face.

Harold wants to tell her about the rucksack dream. In fact there are many things he wants to tell her, but he realises that if he does he will lose control and he does not want to create a scene here in the ward. He is not sure that either of them could cope with that. They have to be strong now.

At the same time though, he feels the time left to them stealing away, just as the ship in his dream did, taking with it the first in a long line of familiar props and supports.

He leans forward awkwardly and puts his lips close to her ear. 'I enjoyed washing your feet, love,' he says. Her eyes engage with his and, briefly, as they hold each others' gaze, everything else drops away. It is a gift.

Don't thank me, thank the moon's gravitational pull

David Gaffney

Christine was managing the office relocation, an opportunity to take her mind off the break-up with Malcolm. Malcolm, however, was health and safety, and everything had to be approved by him.

She indicated with a polished fingernail the position of the new building but Malcolm moaned, shook his head and did nervy jazz hands.

'You've forgotten something vital. The building's relationship to where staff live.'

Christine explained about public transport.

'I was wondering whether it's east or west. I only ever work west of where I live, so that on the way to and from work the sun is never in my eyes.'

'But you come to work on the tube.'

'I have a strong sense of the planet. Even underground I know where I am in relation to the sun.'

She agreed to go with him to a cellar bar so he could demonstrate this skill, and it did explain something. The time he'd consulted a compass before making love, claiming the moon's gravitational pull enhanced his performance, he'd been lying.

Music like ours never dies

David Gaffney

Marion said the article could have been written with me in mind, and I riffled through the supplement and there it was: *Losing it - the Bay City Rollers story.*

The Rollers had everything, but threw it all away. They were egos on legs, emotionally cramped, and manager Tam Patton had a sinister, seamy undertow that eventually destroyed them.

Marion was right. Their story was my story. I was self-obsessed, vain, and paid slipshod attention to Marion's needs. The Bay City Rollers were encoded in me. And Tam Patton? He represented my father. Emotions were un-silted, tears fell on Les McKeon's face, and when Marion returned from her run, I hugged her close.

'Darling, I will never allow us to become the Bay City Rollers.'

She flipped Les over. '*This* is the article I meant.'

EMOTIONAL INFIDELITY, it said, above a picture of a man and woman on a park bench.

Alone, I drew a penis jutting out of the man's trousers and a moustache on the woman. That's what the rollers would have done. What matters is the moment, not everlasting fame.

Away day

David Gaffney

Imagine you are happy. Picture it. You, happy. It can be you, yes. You can be happy, like everyone else. Picture it now. You, a happy person, doing happy things, without a care in the world. Have you got it? Can you see yourself? What are you doing? Don't tell me, I know. You are in the countryside. You are with friends and family, the people you love. It's a sunny day. You are sharing food and drink – wine, even. You are drinking from a paper cup, a tablecloth is laid on the grass.

It is a picnic. You are having a picnic.

Everybody's idea of happiness involves a picnic. A picnic has everything a human being needs. If there were more picnics, the world would be a happier place. And what do our clients want from us but happiness? Isn't that why they come here? Why the health service contracts us to deliver the service?

Next month the clinical psychology team are going on a picnic. Details are attached, along with a map. Please wear appropriate shoes and clothing.

Celia's mum's rat

David Gaffney

I was alone, away from home, and bored, so I lay on the hotel bed and scrolled through the names in my mobile phone. It was then I came across the strange entry. Celia's mum's rat.

I had no idea Celia's mother owned a rat. And if Celia's mother owned a rat, why had she felt the need to buy it a mobile phone? And why had I at some point needed the rat's number, and needed it frequently enough to enter it into the phone's memory? Or, rather, felt a need to know that if the rat called, I would know who it was. Maybe at some point I had decided to avoid the rat's calls or at least wanted time to prepare an excuse as to why I wouldn't be able to assist the rat. Yet surely, if Celia's mum's rat were important enough to own its own phone, the rat would have a name? After all, we didn't call Celia's mum's boyfriend, Celia's mum's boyfriend. We called him Raymond.

I imagined the sleek, smug-faced rodent lying on a miniature chaise longue, the mobile clamped to its ear, squeaking away to other rats with similar luxurious accessories. Budgies have mirrors, hamster have wheels, what do rats have? Phones. Was there a computerised system to translate the rat's squeaks into rudimentary requests? Like food, bedding, water? Handling maybe?

I looked about me at the bleak hotel room. The clock said 11.30. Celia's mum's rat might feel a sudden desire to be handled at any time. Celia's mum and Raymond might be out. My phone would ring and the robot voice would say I WANT YOU TO HANDLE ME NOW, PLEASE.

It was a chilling thought. I turned off my phone and tried to sleep, but the idea of the rat was adhesive. The phone would ring, the demand would be made, and I would drop everything. To assist Celia's mum's rat was my purpose in life.

The Night of Nights, 1948

Seán Burke

For the nocturne, night, at its depth, has no corners, horizons or circumference: a home with a sole inhabitant in which all else abides. The world hovering above a silence not docile but watchful. Something monstrous brought to it by the vestiges of light; something presaged by the seeping dawn. The earth hath bubbles; the sky is not black but slate. Soon it will be filled with idols that have mouths but do not speak; legs but do not walk.

Insomnia awaits the world.

'*J'est un autre.*' He crossed the still ground, the silent shrub toward an abode of stones. As he walked into the great immensity of *things*, he felt as though he was walking into himself. But still something other always remained in all its terrible weight. '*Il y a.*'

That hour before the hour; the dawn before dawn. Somewhere, something stirs. But not within his vision. These ancestral plains; the distant mountain range – an immense masonry without mortar, a colossal design without a designer. Here he could conjure spectres, figures, bid them come and go. Come hither, ghost, brother, double. I have myself come of age in a barren place: plateaus and shades.

He was now in thickets that craved wary walking. The first light began to pool around the foot of the distant mountain, revealing a balleh and water.

A figure not of his summoning for it could hold its visible form: a boy of the Guban filling a pitcher from the balleh. '*Comme lui je me consume.*'

Lanky, swift-eyed and shy, this thing, a bare, forked animal of some fifteen years. It eyed him with distrust and fascination. To run would involve the loss of the pitcher. So, it turned half-toward the pool and the task at hand so as to track his slow, solemn approach.

The boy cupped his hands, drank from the balleh, washed the dust from his face. He too drank from his hands, talked of ordinary things – the impending rain, the prospect of breeze, the nearest town. The boy spoke a dialect familiar to him. Slowly they walked north together, easily evolving a middle tongue. He told him he was 'Prince Tahir of Somalia'.

'Your father must be a King!' The boy had accepted that he was a man of status upon seeing the gold tooth. Perhaps, even, he ascribed to it some magical power or saw it as an insignia of one of the gods too numerous or singular to name.

'My father is on high, holding the urn of doom. I have two elder brothers.'

The mountains resounded just below human hearing. It was not a call or a question. It wasn't even a humming. It was dire, imprecation, brutal, implacable facticity: '*il y a.*'

'Do you hear the low murmur?'

The boy replied in firm, steady tones. 'My father says that if you listen to the mountains, they will drive you mad.'

'Boy - your master's name?'

'Mr Evelyn Herbert.'

'His occupation?'

'Leopard skins, junipers, other things. For shipping from Berbera.'

He asked the boy for directions to Berbera and its port. 'One hour straight ahead, then two hours away from the noon sun.' The boy would head west to the mansion of Mr Evelyn Herbert.

He liked the boy, his secret, happy smile.

They rested beside a shallow watercourse which had become a bed of red sand during the fiery harshness of the *jilaal* season. They entered a dense thicket of thorny bushes which called for wary walking. The thorns might grow as high as three inches and could pierce even a combat boot.

The boy asked of Hargeysa and then of Ethiopia's Harar, of the mysteries of that closed city. He answered with commonplaces that were nonetheless exotic to this boy of the

Guban. 'Some call it the city of the Saints. Many, too, believe it the fourth city of Islam - after Mecca, Medina and Jerusalem.'

The boy talked of a 14-year-old-girl he wished to marry in a few years and of how his master's pay allowed him to save to gain the approval of his *rēr*.

He ran a pianist's hand through the boy's sprawling hair. 'Your master pays you well, boy?'

'He is generous and kind. The work is not hard. Only this gathering of water. I clean once and cook three times a week. I unload deliveries and bring drinks to his bed, to his balcony, his study. For his parties I walk three hours to Berbera. I buy from the markets and an automobile is paid to drive me back.'

'And no more work than that?'

'At night,' the boy said, looking amused and bashful, 'I must sometimes go to the local village to get company for him and his friends. One man, he is so grey and fat, he bangs his glass on the table and shouts at me. 'Anis – Cunt!' 'Anis – Cunt!'. The men - such fools.'

The boy got up and started through the thicket. Still giggling, he negotiated an expert path between the thorny bushes.

He put an encouraging arm around the boy's shoulder.

'I say no bad of my master. But I come in with drinks last week. One is vomiting on the carpet saying 'fuck, it was something I ate earlier'. Another has a woman's mouth inside his trousers and he is farting, and snoring so loud. And one of the women has my master's thing out and she is thumping it on the table but it just flops and looks sore and so little and he gets dressed again.'

The boy went down heavily, the pitcher still clutched to his chest. A thorn had cut through his shoulder flesh; another must have lodged into his lower back. Anis's mouth was wide open but his twitching body emitted no sound. A scream there was when he pulled up Anis's left leg and rammed it down on an adjacent thorn. The thorn went right through his ankle. Now the boy was impaled. He checked his clothes and hands for blood, then stripped naked. He awaited the boy's blood: it was slow in coming; no main artery had been severed.

He wondered awhile whether to experiment or leave the boy for carrion. The boy *just* might extricate himself. He began hacking off his toes. The boy's screams were all of a piece with the world; a hyena calling, the unanswerable cry of a bird.

A fluent flash of the blade across the boy's throat sufficed to create the corpse that already presaged its return. '*Corps remagnetisé.*' 'I' cannot murder an Other for 'I' am already another. Such is most minute self-mutilation; drawing blood from a palm, crushing an insect underfoot.

He drank from the pitcher. He washed his knife and concealed it in the thicket. Buzzards would circle in the noon sun; hyenas would follow. Nothing would remain but bone and none would venture these blistering paths before nightfall.

The thickets gave way to a plain of red dust and then to dust mingled with lava. He was west now of the mountains and in sight of the low hills where he would find the abode of Mr Evelyn Herbert.

I

Herbert's mansion was not large but neither did it fail to speak of grandeur amidst its desolation. It was three storeys high with scorched balustrades, and stunted verandas. Its grounds were defined by a ruined gate and a fence that was merely a dozen lengths of barbed wire. A glacial Janus, shaded by acacia trees, was the sole statue in the garden. Beyond the jagged perimeter, the acacia trees receded before tall tamarisks. To the north-facing back of the mansion was a circular tower of luminous white with a charred wooden door. Beside it was chained a moon-coloured hound which sprung to its feet whenever he came within thirty yards of the tower. There was as much of fear as aggression in the beast. It shivered as it growled in the afternoon sun.

Observing Herbert's mansion and its owner's movements, he had the curious sense that he too was being observed. Herbert appeared to do no work. A military wagon bore him six large boxes of supplies. Come sundown, two military men and another in a beige suit drank with Herbert on the verandah. They drove and returned noisily at midnight with two seemingly disgruntled local women. The following day Herbert spent drinking alone on the verandah, alternating between listening to the wireless and classical music on his gramophone.

Toward dusk, he sauntered up the path, saluted Herbert as he sat motionless and without occupation on the verandah, his eyes absorbing the barren half-lights, the scrubbed hills. Herbert did not return the gesture but got to his feet. Some five minutes later, he opened the door.

Three decades separated the two men. Herbert was an inch the shorter at 5'8'. He was bespectacled, broad shouldered with pencil-thin limbs and a grotesquely distended belly. Herbert weighed this young man for his stately bearing and a gaze that was dreamy yet burning with some insatiable desire. The other looked at him as might a gentleman's outfitter. He gauged that his trousers hovered an inch above leather sandals and that it was with braces rather than a belt that he accommodated his paunch. He noted that Herbert wore a gold wedding ring, surmised (correctly) that he was a widower without issue. He face was bloated and grotesquely mottled with drink. From behind his glasses, he peered hazily into the middle distance, muttered some dismay at the sunset.

'My name is Prince Tahir Gass.'

'Prince of what?'

'A portion of the interior. My life has been divided between an academy in Harar and a palace of mirrors in Hargeysa.'

'There is indeed something of dignity in your bearing. Come in, Prince whatever.'

Gass followed into the hallway, past a study and kitchen table bearing welters of paperwork, empty spirit bottles, cigar and cigarette ends folded into the table or trodden into the marble floor. He was gestured into the uncluttered drawing room.

'My bloody bearer, stupid, adorable ass of a boy – I don't know whether he has gallivanted off with that girl of his or been left to the mercy of the wild.'

'I could be of service, should it please you, sir. Until such time as your bearer returns.'

Herbert contemplated a cigar but lit a Sweet Afton cigarette. 'Fucking good smoke, these – I get them shipped over,' he said, holding the yellow packet aloft. He poured raw gin into a murky tumbler, sat down in the front room and considered.

'I suppose you'll do as well as any, Prince whatever. One's needs are limited at this time of life.'

II

For three days Herbert was content to live on alcohol and food spooned straight from tins. Gass's only duty was to mix gin, Pimms and soda upon the banging of the gong which signalled Herbert's awakening. On one occasion, so bad was his tremor, Gass had to raise the glass to Herbert's lips. The desperation in his eyes was as luminous as that of a man with a blade held to his throat. Alcohol was the master of Mr Evelyn Herbert, and Gass was surprised to see how brutal and jealous was its reign.

Gass would study and memorise choice passages of the *Koran* during his time here. He would also make of his body a devotional text. While Herbert drank and read or listened to music on his favoured, west-facing verandah, Gass read in the shade of an acacia tree near the circular tower. He began to detest the moon-coloured hound. *That cur knows something: it shivers with apprehension.* Unbearable, too, were the parties. '*Vous êtes de faux nègres.*'

'No one should know of your presence here,' Herbert had stipulated. Gass welcomed seclusion but loathed the twice-weekly parties: the laughter, drunkenness, the protracted, garbled valedictions of the guests as they left for their automobiles, the persona his master adopted for these English clowns. The Evelyn Herbert he knew was a man given to silence, melancholy, introspection and a few hours of intellectual discussion come dusk. Ruined in body, his mind was yet that of a master without slaves. He was entitled to the oblivion of his gin even if, as on more than one occasion, he had fouled his trousers leaving Gass to shoulder him to the bathroom, undress, bathe, dry and put him abed. Far less hygienic were these despicable gatherings.

On a quiet March evening, the rains began. 'We have entered the *Gu* season,' Gass observed as they sat in the drawing room. 'The season of marriages, contests, the settlement of disputes and of rites of passage. Adolescent boys are subjected to tests, humiliations, and trials through which they must pass if they are to become men and worthy of women.'

Gass described the various rituals associated with the harsh fires of *jilaal* from which they had only now emerged into the redemptive *Gu* season of rains, of the dry *hagga'* when vegetation shrivels almost to nothing and of the blessed rains of *dayr*. Gass spoke of Ramadhan's most subtle miracle - the 'Night of Nights' when the water in the pitchers tastes sweeter, mysteries unveil themselves and the songs of nightbirds resonate with the music of the spheres.

'It occurs at the end of the Gu season,' Gass explained. 'In approximately eleven weeks.'

'Be so good as to calculate the precise date for me.'

That night they talked of Shakespeare, of ancient Greece, of monotheism and its displacement of the collective rituals of musical frenzy, prophesy and transport. Herbert expressed quiet admiration for Gass's erudition.

'Oh, but sir, I was cunningly taught by two men; one of the most compendious knowledge, another of inexhaustible wisdom. I have read less than four hundred books in my twenty-eight years: all western and deemed of high canonical value. From other texts I was given selected passages whose value transcended that of the work as a whole. My current study of the *Koran* is my first untutored adventure of reading.'

'You were not brought up in the Muslim faith?'

'In ritual, yes, through history and shadow. But from me the sacred text was withheld indefinitely. My father dreamt that I should first assimilate the wisdom of the west and then bring it under the sway of the prophetic wisdom. He wished me to form a revolutionary synthesis of Greek philosophy, Judaism, Christianity and the occult; to know and to return to the West its ultimate *fin de siècle décadence*. Thenceforth, I am to subject all to the sternest ordinances of Islamic teaching.'

'If realised, how will this dream insert itself onto the plane of reality?'

'In the gradual, fractured manner of a genuine revolution. I must visit Tiger Bay in Cardiff.'

'Tiger Bay,' Herbert mused. 'I have shipped many exports through there. Why choose this now declining port?'

'Haile Selassie uses a house there as a European haven. I have seen his face in all manner of things – in clouds, in rocks, in termite mounds, on the surface of the *ballehs* and gullies from which I have drunk. Tiger Bay is also refuge to a good many of my own people.'

'And at this meeting you would be Selassie's enemy?'

'Yes, I would assassinate this false man of peace. When in Cardiff he is unguarded, unwary even.'

Gass broke off, admiring the lacework on the dress shirt Herbert had provided for him.

'Quite a dream, indeed,' said Herbert. 'Perhaps your asylum here is among the manifestations of this dream.' Herbert drained his glass and climbed the broad, crimson-carpeted staircase. 'The Night of Nights,' he said as he opened his bedroom door.

III

The next morning, Herbert washed, shaved, applied scent, put cream through his thinning, sandy-brown hair and emerged in a suit and tie. Only then did he call for his ibis-headed ashtray and morning drink. He dictated more than a dozen letters relating that due to ill-health and the loss of his manservant, he would neither attend social gatherings nor entertain guests. Daily visits were made by a consular doctor, he reassured one and all. His condition was not serious, but required a prolonged period of rest before a return to Britain of some six months.

The following week, Herbert worked through the mounds of paperwork that made his study virtually impossible to negotiate, yet alone clean. Gin bottle in hand, he would emerge waxen and exhausted. 'Pilfering on the river,' he said one afternoon. 'Pilfering, pilfering, pilfering – they cannot be trusted an inch.'

Herbert was utterly stupefied that night. Gass guided him to master bedroom, laid him down. 'Now I might do it.'

He went into the utility room, found a hammer and a set of two-inch nails. He undressed, tiptoed to the north-west side of the mansion. The moon-coloured hound stirred from its vigilant sleep. It barked, it growled. It shivered, it yelped. And then, throat slit from ear to ear, suffered no more. Naked, Gass unchained the carcass and nailed it paw-by-paw to the rain-softened wooden door of the circular tower.

The following morning, Gass brought two drinks to Herbert's bed. 'There is bad news,' he said. 'My words will not serve.'

Herbert drank the first negroni as he dressed. The second he took to the garden. Uncommonly bright in step, he approached the circular tower.

'The dog crucifix,' he said, as another might 'flat tyre' or 'the garden is waterlogged'

'Shall I bury the hound?'

'Leave it to those who eat monkey flesh and lizards,' Herbert said imperiously.

IV

A strange gleam came into Herbert's eyes toward the middle of the Gu season. He cleared his study and made merry bonfires of his paperwork. Merlot had become his drink of choice and with it his mood mellowed. No longer did he end his days in a stupor. His face was less bloated, his colour had come down and he was stronger in gait. He devoted his mornings to coffee and personal correspondence. At noon, he would sip on his first glass of wine and spend hours at the piano on which he would compose simple, lilting airs.

The dispiriting ritual of the evening meal underwent a transformation. Through his consular or military friends, Herbert had engaged the services of two homespun catering operations. The meals were light, served in numerous small dishes, and slowly consumed as Herbert paused over a bottle of good claret. On one such evening, Herbert had consumed no alcohol during the daylight hours.

'Nazism is vanquished,' he said, 'and the secular alternative offered by Marxism will not satisfy the still-living religious instinct in the wake of the death of God. Islam may

87

well fill the void onto which our century has opened. God died in terrible agony at Auschwitz and his demise was marked with an infallible sign. In the fourth century, Constantine I saw a cross in the sky bearing the insignia 'in this sign, conquer'. What Constantine saw was without doubt a mushroom cloud produced by natural forces. Three years ago, a mushroom cloud appeared over Hiroshima. Between two mushroom clouds, then, separated by 1621 years, the entire epoch of Christendom unfolds and closes. We have lived through the most appalling decade in the history of humankind. And yet we have lived and would live on. Is this not enough to amaze eternity?'

'I do not believe the great wars have yet been fought,' responded Gass with dreamy conviction.

Herbert raised his wine glass, examined it as might a lapidary a gemstone. 'Every drink has led me to you, the one which marks the end of a sequence commenced at the end of the Great War.'

From that valediction on, he washed down his copious cigarettes and ceremonial cigars with some thirty cups of sweet tea a day. He read little now but dedicated himself to experiments with synchronic scales and the computation of ever higher prime numbers

Herbert's thoughts had turned toward the Infinite. It explained those long hours he'd spent simply looking to the horizon as if for its beyond.

V

As the Gu season drew towards its close, the rain stopped and the air was light, cleansed and invigorating at higher altitudes. Herbert received official visitors, some consular, some military, others representing him in his complex tangle of business and investment interests. Satisfied by his construal of the twentieth sura, which tells of Musa and the prostration of the magicians, Gass took to day-long walks. He passed through dead forests, gathered frankincense and myrrh on the lower ground, plucked juniper on the cool heights, crept stone over alluvial stone, looked below for his quarry. All nature felt charged, brewing, expectant as if the stones and gullies, the mountains, watercourses and even the dead forests, were building toward the Night of Nights.

His quarry he'd killed at dawn. He'd pulled out the imposhume or sack-like cyst of congealed blood from the small royal antelope, *neotragus pygmaeus*. By mid-afternoon the liquor's hue was burnished into a golden beyond gold, the very form of goldenness itself. He reopened the last of his wounds, pasted each carving with the antelope's liquor, gave his naked leg over to the sun. Blood moved sensuously through his mind, his arteries sang, his head was a-swim with mingled delights: peace overwhelmed. The letters became regal insignia, stigmata; his body, but parchment, surface and scroll. The twenty-ninth and final letter of the name had been inscribed.

VI

The days leading up to the Night of Nights (Gass had taken to calling it the Night of Power) were routine. Visits had come to a close. Herbert had travelled as far along the road to infinity as his energy or patience would permit.

'30029', he declared. '30+029=59. I am 59 years of age. This charmless auspice combined with renewed lassitude brought my perfectly needless occupation to a close.'

Gass spent the daylight hours of May 29th absorbed in easy rituals that were also rituals of ease. By sunset, the downstairs was an intoxication of mingled scents. Herbert sipped with seeming appreciation from a glass of sweetened water. Being did not sit so heavily with his master of late. Herbert had fasted, drunk much water and consumed a considerable quantity of purgatives over the previous three days and nights.

'The Night of Nights would seem to be the six hundred and second of that work in which the time of narrative repels the hour of death. The ratio 602:1001 has no special privilege or property beyond sharing 7 as a factor.'

'It is either blasphemy or ignorance (perhaps they are one and the same) to assume continuity between the cosmological genius of Allah and the sublunary cunning of Shahrazad,' countered Gass. A strange melancholy and loneliness came over him as he brought two large tureens of water to the boil. The sun was on the verge of setting; from the garden, came a gentle, unwitnessing breeze.

Herbert lit a cigarette, dragged heavily, and blew a sequence of five smoke rings, which tailed each other onto the marble floor. He then spoke. 'You have known me as an ancestor of the aristocratic Herbert line, as a man of not inconsiderable means and as a patriot. One detail alone is true. I am in fact the only child of a post office clerk in Clerkenwell, London. Here I am a man of great wealth: in the City of London I would be a bankrupt. After Potsdam, and with the Allied Commission, my creditors will altogether sooner write off my debts than pursue me to this desolate place.'

'I have known you as a Prince from the City of Hargeysa who seeks an Islamic revolution. This may be true in part or whole; it may be entirely false: I have no desire to make any such discriminations. Rather, I have extended a certain hospitality to you under the masquerade of service. I have amused myself with the unfolding of master-slave dialectic. I wished to witness the inevitable, indeed evolutionary, usurpation of the ever-more dependent master by the increasingly resourceful slave.'

Herbert passed across an envelope containing a consular letter which was both a passport and employment reference along with a one-way ticket to Cardiff and a bountiful remittance in sterling.

'Your ship sails at 12:30 tomorrow. You will leave this house by dawn having erased every trace of your presence.'

It was just after eleven when, having polished a tall-stemmed glass to a fine sheen, Gass fetched up the requested claret. The servant summoned his master to the window. The stars were indeed brighter; the sky had opened wide. The seals had been broken. Long-held secrets and testimonies were abroad, audible to those elect of belief. The layers of meaning under encryptions shone forth in their primordial purity. It was the night of revelation. Even in the mountains, he knew, the falcons called *saker* stayed claw-to-ground, watchful as ever, but settled and docile. Gass thought, too, of the lanner birds and sparrows, idle but expectant in their nests.

Herbert respected his companion's reverie. When finally he spoke, his voice was changed. It was as though another spoke behind him. 'As of 1900, the ratio pertaining between those who lived and those who had died was approximately 1:1. The living are now but a curious, out-ranked species of the dead.'

Gass browsed amongst Herbert's belongings, selected a pocket watch, and cufflinks of gold and silver. Into two light brown leather suitcases, he packed five of Herbert's suits, ten of his shirts and four ties. He left the bedroom window open by an inch. His search of the circular tower revealed it to be little more than a vast spiral of paperwork. He fastened a gold watch to his left wrist, gathered a spectacularly embossed copy of *Paradise Lost* and some ladies' jewelry of indeterminate value.

He stripped his bed, placed its linen on top of the suitcases in the hallway. Any farewell to Mr Evelyn Herbert was out of the question. He looked, for the last time at his master, seated facing away from him, his chair moved closer to the window.

So ended the longest period of relative serenity it was either man's destiny to experience.

VII

It wasn't yet dawn when Gass came in sight of the Berbera and its port. Even then he knew it only from the tang of brine in his nostrils and a few disappointed harbour lights. He had walked unaware that he was walking through so much dust, stubble, sere and spent stone. For this desolate coastal stretch had British Somaliland been created. Along with Aden, the British had twin gatekeeper ports for the Red Sea which was vital to their trade with the Indian colonies. Close on one third of Somaliland's male population died in the resistance, but much was learned about the power of Islam to unite a people. In rallying the Dervishes to a jihad, though, Sayyid Muhammad should have called to a global Islam.

The light broadened as he walked through a dead forest of bottle and dragon trees to gain the foreshore. He rested beside a city of castles built by crabs on the beach. The colours of this beautiful dawn – *his dawn* - all rhymed. '*A noir, E blanc, I rouge, O bleu, U vert*'. If we humans signify with the language of words, Allah signifies through the language of things. *Il y a.*

In an embarkation point toilet cubicle, he examined the inner side of his left leg. The letters were as uniform as he could have expected, the gold dye evenly spread: 'Prince Tahir of Somalia.'

'*L'esprit est autorité, il veut que je sois en Occident,*' he whispered to himself on deck. His body was taut, thin and primed; his eyes milky with psychosis. He was stalwart and straight-backed, light-skinned in a black pinstripe suit, his hair falling in ringlets onto a starched shirt.

His task awaited, called him to its unfolding. Looking out at the Gulf of Aden as the ship's engines began to rumble, he thought of Alexander of Macedonia, of how in a moment of visionary transport or Oedipal repugnance, he'd reversed his father's counsel to proceed westward and ordered his armies advance to the East at the Danube. So, on a heartbeat, turned the history of civilisation. Alexander would not have been mired in Asia, 'Rome' would have become *Alexandria*, 'Paris' *Olympia* and 'Christianity' neither a word or concept, let alone the dominant world religion. He tried to think forward to his fate, to the world-historical individual he would become. But his mind still returned to his last conversation with Evelyn Herbert.

'"I owe a cock to Asclepius" – such were Socrates' last words. Asclepius was the Greek god of medicine. When cured, a Greek was expected to sacrifice a cock in his honour .'

'So Socrates had come to see life as a disease,' Gass inferred.

'Quite so, my brilliant Prince.' Glass by glass, he eased the claret down his master's throat.

'Kill me as you killed my boy.'

'Not quite as I killed your boy, sir. Raise your arms from the tureens and hold the blade to your wrist as if you were to slit it yourself. Then will I force your hand to the task.'

Gass felt some resistance in Herbert's right hand as he removed his wedding ring, emblem, for this mercy killer of status, emblem for both of mourning. There was no such rebellion when Gass took the knife to bloated veins, the blood now draining, then oozing, until it seeped like light brushed on light, or the compacted air we see as frost.

Postscript

Tahir Gass's destiny was to fork in 1956. In Cardiff, by 1952, he had made fruitless alliance with the black activist Michael X who was intent on becoming Britain's Malcom X. That year, Gass committed the first of two murders which were remarkable for their mixture of calculated financial gain and the evident pleasure (from which sexual expression was entirely absent) carved into the victims' faces and necks. Found guilty of the latter homicide by reason of insanity, he was confined for an indefinite period to Broadmoor hospital. In 1956, he was covertly discharged onto a nocturnal boat whose unproven destination makes his fate not that of one but two men.

In the first, he was disembarked in northern Spain. A picaresque sequence of murders and robberies took him from Bilbao to San Sebastian, to Turin, Milan, Verona, Bologna and Naples. Back in Somalia by 1958, Gass took up residence at the mansion of Mr Eveyln Herbert and was worshipped by the local villagers as a god. Beyond wealth and erudition, the fact that he held audience with a skeleton added to the awe and reverence in which he was held. He is said to have sacrificed himself to the greater god on the Night of Nights, 1998.

According to the second, he was taken to Berbera and deposited under military guard ten miles to the south. Suffering from advanced tuberculosis, he managed to scramble and crawl the seven miles to Herbert's mansion. Too unwell to eat any of the tinned food, he prayed for rain. The Gu season arrived a week late and he died of dehydration.

In both destinies, at the point of death, he was granted the reassurance of an unspectacular symmetry. That he had sought out Mr Evelyn Herbert did not rule out the possibility, in death as in life, that Herbert had also summoned him.

For K.H.B.

The Kiss

(After Chekhov's story of the same name)

Martin Sorrell

Reg is standing in his kitchen, looking out at the sinking sun as he dries the mugs he used to take a brew half an hour before to the workmen digging up the pavement.

The day's gone sour. He reckons he knows what it is that's caused the damage, the thing he's done, but he doesn't accept there had to be consequences. He feels he's been stranded.

The workmen are about to pack up for the day. They started at breakfast time, directly outside the house where Reg has the ground-floor flat. Two Balfour Beatty lorries arrived, one big, the other, smaller, trailing a cylinder on wheels, a generator in fact. Several men, tattoos, ear rings, leapt to the ground in their yellow over-jackets. The buried pipe-work needed renewing, the leaflet through everyone's letterbox had warned. The present stuff not only was ancient, but a health hazard, given that it was made of lead – something that doesn't surprise Reg, since this town is substantially 1920s and 30s, expanded to house the labour force that found employment in its single industry, a railway carriage works which was built on unprofitable flatlands. Now, where the works once sprawled, developments of semis and fake Tudor detached homes, kit-built in a fortnight, are the replacements.

In Reg's part of town, plastic pipes have to go in. The Balfour Beatties' job today has been to take up the paving slabs. Reg was surprised this morning at how easy that was, no pickaxes, no levering, just a couple of men lowering what looked like a large magnet onto the slabs, taking hold of grab handles, lifting. Up they came, light as Lego. Reg stood watching. He asked how the devil it worked. It's a great new piece of kit, they told him, made in China. A child could operate it, piece of piss. And there's no bad effect on the lower back, no Health and Safety issues. It works by suction, one grey-haired worker said, gives a great blow job. Reg asked if they could use a brew. When he brought out their teas, the grey-haired workman invited Reg to have a go on his magnet.

***

Reg has moved here, where Lancing edges into Worthing, because it's about the only affordable place in the area that took his fancy. Brighton, the obvious choice, he didn't take to; brittle sort of place and, let's face it, effeminate. Anyway it was unaffordable. The flat he's bought instead is modest, part of a terraced house six roads back from the shoreline. Nearer the sea, prices get ridiculous.

The reason for his move south was to be nearer his son Alan, his wife Jemma and their two children. They live close to Preston Park on the north edge of Brighton, in a large Edwardian property. Reg has wondered if this house, even Brighton itself, might be just a stopgap, because he's not too sure they're settled. His daughter-in-law, in particular, seems restless. She's said more than once that she doesn't much care for the south coast. Nor has Alan expressed disagreement.

Reg hopes that Alan's job, which brought them to Sussex, will keep them here. Perhaps soon Jemma can find something too. A part-time museum post, maybe. Reg wants them to settle properly. He's become very attached to his two grandchildren. He's no longer fussed about their strange names, Imogen and Oliver. Getting close to them has caught him unawares. He's never been one for Nearest and Dearest. The wide canvas, mankind writ large, that's where he's at home. Balfour Beatties, for example. Male fellowship to go with the tea. When 'Imo' and then 'Ollie' appeared, his first reaction on both occasions was that he didn't want to know. But he checked himself quickly, and each time forced himself over to the hospital in Oxford. What he saw caught him amidships. Triumphant mother, flushed father, and packages the size of his fist, first one then the other eighteen months later. Two faces, a hundred years old, the world-weariness of the newborn... But most of all, each time it was Jemma. He couldn't recall ever being got in the guts quite like that by someone's smile.

Now, today, in his kitchen, unhappy, Reg is adrift on memories. The days before Lancing. How he travelled from Birmingham down to Oxford to see them, sometimes by train but usually on the coach. He preferred the coach to the train. Quieter and cheaper, no young families, no space for them to charge around. On the Oxford run, you got two kinds of people: serious readers, science journals or books about the ancient world; and then people like him, who nodded off, their tabloids slipping to the floor. Reg could do the round trip, Birmingham and back in a day comfortably, and spend what people like to call 'quality time' with the kids. Mostly, in the first three years, he went on his own, but, until the cancer defeated her stoicism, his wife Heather went too. Ollie and Imo were fast turning into recognisable human things, fun to be with, lovely to look at. Lovelier than their parents and certainly lovelier than him. He reckons that they must be throwbacks, a couple of generations up the line. Perhaps in an old tobacco tin he'll find one day some foxed photos to prove it, a smart soldier with moustaches, a young woman in white blouse and high-waist skirt, looking seriously at the camera.

When the family left Oxford for Brighton, because of his son's new job, it became physically impossible for Reg to visit them in a single day from Smethwick. He never wanted to stay overnight in their house. Of course they said that he was very welcome to, especially after Heather died, but he reckoned they didn't want it any more than he did. Reg likes privacy when he has to get up in the night; he doesn't want people hearing.him splashing around in their bathroom. So the four visits he did make before the move down south, he stayed in Hove in a B&B with en-suite. Money well spent.

He considers himself well established in his new life. He's been going over regularly to Brighton, following routines that please everyone. Bus along the coast, one change in Western Road, an hour and twenty minutes door to door. Sometimes his arrival's been timed to allow him to meet the children coming out of school and give Jemma a chance to do some work in her study. Ollie and Imo like that – for better reasons, Reg wants to think, than the obvious one of treats on the way home. Sweets, comics. He hasn't been against modest treats because they've given him the chance to teach the little ones good manners. No eating, no reading in the street. Wait until you get indoors. Learn some self-control. He doesn't care if it's not entirely rational. It's his rule, and there it is. Reg may not be an educated man, but his values are sound. They were forged in firmer times. He reckons he might have made a good teacher, or at least a good disciplinarian, pretty much the same thing, or ought to be.

Routinely, Reg has taken the children to the park. Slides, roundabouts, swings. Predictable but surprisingly good fun. The park's a short walk away, and has two valuable plusses. The first is the ice-cream van that seems to live there. On each visit its innards are plundered. Reg sometimes gets something for himself, and enjoys it more than he expects. The second plus is the railway line that runs just beyond the bottom railings. Bearing their plunder, the three of them position themselves for the best view of the trains. In reality, just the one, because Reg knows that novelty soon becomes boredom, for him as well. Ollie, true boy that he is, unfailingly gets excited. Reg thinks that despite what some people like to believe, in a boy's blood trains whistle, planes whoosh, cars crash. Imo can't connect, but she mimics her brother with willing good grace.

Saturday, three weeks ago, instead of the usual electric train of three or four carriages, what they heard and then saw was a steamer, a special excursion for nutters and retards. Ollie was beside himself. Imo echoed his excitement without having a clue why. The engine pulling the train was green, Reg recounts, though Ollie, out of control, screams that it was blue like the one in Thomas the Tank Engine, but eight times bigger. Reg won't climb down any more than Ollie, but catching Jemma's eye, realises he must become an adult again. He says sorry, of course he's wrong and Ollie's right. Calmed, Ollie asks Reg, did you drive that engine for your job, or one like it? Reg, a lathe operator all of his working life, lies. Yes, I did, along this very track, and sometimes it was the Royal Train with the Queen waving. He goes on, she was waving with her left hand and holding down her crown with the right, while the Duke of Edinburgh stood picking his nose at a separate window. Ollie is helpless with joy. Reg is learning the power of words.

The most important thing he's discovered with those two kids is the sense of play he didn't have, even as a young boy. And the sinful warmth you get when you're appreciated. To very little children, someone of Reg's years is interesting or funny or both, almost automatically. Nothing much is needed. You pull a weird face and they fall about; if you have a speciality in your repertoire, such as wiggling your ears or yodelling, even better. Both of Reg's tricks make Ollie almost die of laughter. On one occasion, he fell into an asthma attack which for a few minutes was worrying. Reg thinks that Alan finds his antics ill-judged, and not only because of the scare with Ollie. Reg thinks that's fair enough because, regrettably, there are few if any memories for Alan of his dad making him laugh like that when he was small. Jemma is very different. Her childhood was a festival of giving and receiving. It comes easily for her to think her father-in-law a bit of a hoot. I'd never have suspected it of you, she said to him once as he succeeded, more or less, in doing a mime Marcel Marceau made famous. Well well, she said, hidden talents. Her eyes were laughing.

Reg thinks, though, that things have got a lot better between him and his son. Ollie and Imo have smoothed the way. And Alan seems to appreciate Reg's involvement with them all. He's begun to tell his father about his work, even if Reg hasn't been able to understand much. He seems to like it that his father gets on with Jemma. One day of sun and shadows in the garden, while Alan was at work and the children still in school, she opened up and told him about her passion for Chile and that part of the world. She talked about the tribe she lived with for a year high in the Andes, the book she was writing about it before the children.

***

But today, little over an hour ago, wordlessly, everything changed. After Reg had collected Ollie and Imo from school, Alan said they'd got some news, and they thought this was the right time to tell him. Alan asked if his dad fancied a glass of wine, even though it was a bit early for alcohol. He said they'd brought a few cases of very nice wine back from France; there was an interesting Sancerre waiting to be uncorked. Go on then, Reg replied, just a drop. You only live once. Alan fetched the bottle. Cheers, he said. Happy days, said Reg. The wine scorched his throat and chest and tasted not much different from Dettol. What he really needed at this time of day was tea.

He sat there, clasping his glass, thinking, I know what the news is; they're going to tell me Jemma's pregnant. It doesn't surprise him. They were never going to stick at only two children. Three at least, maybe four.

Jemma came in. Reg saw her and Alan exchange glances. She smiled and went into the kitchen to look for some nibbles. Reg put down his glass and said to Alan that he was going for a leak. He left the room, but instead of the understairs toilet he found himself entering the kitchen. As Jemma turned to him with her smile, on an impulse he grabbed hold of her face and kissed her full on the mouth and held her like that until he ran out of breath, and was forced to stop crushing her lips, squeezing her temples, pulling at her hair. Then he went to empty his bladder. He saw that in one hand there was a strand of Jemma'a hair.

He heard Jemma running upstairs. Ollie and Imo had started fighting. Reg tidied himself and went out in the garden, and stood there for a few moments, then went back into the empty sitting room, and dropped into his chair. He heard Alan coming downstairs. He said it was time for his father to go home. Reg said the next bus wasn't for an hour. I'll drive you, said Alan. Let's go.

The journey was silent. Alan made a big thing of concentrating, as he fought the glare of a strong sun made more blinding by the insects smeared across the windscreen. When they arrived at the junction of Reg's road, Alan put on the handbrake and told Reg the news that they were going to tell him back in Brighton. It wasn't what Reg had thought. It was that Alan had had the offer of a position it was difficult to turn down, if not impossible. He'd been head-hunted by MIT in Boston, USA. He and Jemma had been agonising about it for an age. There was under a week left to decide. But, well, the conditions, the money, the prestige. Alan reached across Reg and opened his door. He said goodbye quickly, adjusting the car's sun visor. There'd been no mention of anything else. Reg sensed that now wasn't the time to check if the plans for tomorrow still stood.

***

Reg finishes drying the workmen's mugs. He stays where he is, leaning with both hands on the table, watching the sun disappear. Then it comes to him. What Alan's told him is a damn lie. They've already made their decision. They'll be going to the USA. He reckons the MIT contract's already signed sealed and delivered. Those two have been beating their brains trying to find a way of transferring the responsibility away from themselves, and that silly business with the kiss has done the trick. He reckons that his unexpected surge of the old energy in their kitchen has done them one huge favour.

He's certainly not going to apologise. He'll wait for them to get in touch if they choose. They know where to find him. As for the USA, they're welcome to it. He's staying put in Lancing. He can make himself a decent little life here. He's getting to like the blandness of the place. On the new estates, there'll be lots of people like him to meet. And there's plenty of activity, if you know where to look, and there are the one offs, like the pipe-laying today. Reg is disappointed the work by his front gate has taken only a day. The Balfour Beatties have told him that tomorrow, Tuesday, they'll be setting up camp outside number 117. Reg thinks, quick as that? Life these days.

Still, those workmen will want their tea. First thing in the morning, Reg will take them their mugs, plus one for himself, which he'll drink as he watches the Chinese device suck up more pavement. Later, say three o'clock, he'll bring out slices of the cake he's bought to take to Brighton for Ollie and Imo to put candles on. Tomorrow is his eightieth birthday.

Then, once the workmen have packed up, he'll go down to the seafront. Perhaps the tide will be out. He likes it that on this stretch of coast the sea recedes so far, uncovering fields of sand. Maybe he'll get the bus along to Worthing and sit on the pier. A satisfying pier, unfussy, understated, better than Brighton's. From the seats and benches that line each side of the partition running down its deck, on a bright morning the best is to face eastwards and look at the Seven Sisters; and in the afternoon switch to the other side and watch the setting sun glance off the Beach Hotel, where colourful flags sometimes catch the breeze.

Mulling over tomorrow's options, Reg decides that, yes, that's how he'll finish the day. Any birthday cake left over he'll take to offer round. It all depends on the weather, naturally. The forecast is good, but things can change.

What You Know

Andrew Caink

Christo farted all night in the corner. Deep trumpets of garlic and crap sausages. On the other side, Dimiter snored like the tide, each gurgling wave a little louder until the peak, a moment of silence when his weary body hung in the balance, then a crack as his tongue was dislodged and the cycle began again. Milcho didn't write these things down, but he lay in the dark and composed them in his head. And then he was back to thinking about Krasi. Pretty Krasimira, that day in the hills above Sliven, saying 'I'll be the film-star, you write the screenplays,' as she pouted for the bushes. She went to Sofia three years back, chasing an advertisement for models abroad. 'First Italy, then Hollywood,' she said to Milcho, dancing a ruchenitsa round the yard, Baba in the corner smiling as she worked in a cloud of chicken feathers. There were a couple of calls during the first days, then nothing.

'She's fine, she's not just a pretty face,' Baba said.

She had been better at English, always fives out of six at school whereas Milcho was down in the threes, and it showed now. He thought he spoke the language until he got here and the immigration guy barked at him, and he wasn't even English either. Most people here weren't; there were Poles, Ukrainians, Estonians, blacks and Asians. The only sort Milcho hadn't met was the Englishman in Chapter 15 of the Eighth's textbook. They learnt the passage by heart (Krasi did, Milcho cheated): bowler hat, cricket, roast beef and Yorkshire pudding. They hardly saw any English, just the gaffers on site who went in for neither reserve nor bowler hats. They shouted angrily and, if you didn't catch the words, you got the gist from their tone. Milcho would nod, avoid eye contact and hiss at Dimiter, 'What he say?'

Milcho slept eventually and Christo shook him awake early, saying, 'Happy first of March!' He handed round pieces of red and white string. Someone must have sent them over. Milcho tied one round his wrist, marvelling that he could have missed the date. Maria, who slept with the Romanian in the front, she made the coffee sweet and strong, but another sleepless night had him feeling like a van stuck in first gear.

Half an hour later, they stood in the usual place and waited, the sun not yet over the factory opposite. Whatever they made there, the workers ignored the gathering of foreigners on the other side of the road as they changed shifts. There was no sign of the trucks yet. Christo slapped Dimiter on the arm and told him a joke at which they smiled, then went back to sauntering around, studying the pavement, each in his own world. Englishness creeps in. Whatever the day ahead brought, Milcho decided he would blow some money at the internet café in the evening, chat to some friends; that would be his treat.

'Kórva,' a Polish guy muttered and gobbed into the road. The Poles were the largest group. They didn't mix with anyone else. They were all right in ones or twos, but very proud in a pack. There was a hierarchy: the Poles and Ukrainians; they could pass for English on the street. Milcho and his mates were at the bottom with the Romanians; people thought they were gypsies. Poles even had their own red and white shops, sachets of powdered soup and jars of pickles. Milcho found a packet of škembe one time. He was so pleased, like a child. It tasted shit, nothing like Baba's, and Dimiter said it wasn't Bulgarian tripe soup anyway. It was Turkish. It had been a heavy day and Milcho lost it. He waved the packet in Dimiter's face, pointing to the word they'd transliterated as *işkembe*, and Dimiter said it was Turkish; that's where it came from.

There was a Turkish woman at the strawberry-picking farm. Milcho didn't speak to her at first, but she had a mouth like Krasi's and after a bit they chatted quietly as they made their way down the rows. She told him about their food, carpets, Turkish delights, and all the words were Bulgarian. Milcho was furious. He told her about the haiduti, the outlaws running through the mountains, defeating the Turks. He told her that the Turks were the devils in Bulgaria. He told her about the atrocities, the inhuman butchery, so savage that even the English Gladstone objected and the world-famous Oscar Wilde wrote a poem. He told her these things that even schoolchildren in Bulgaria learnt. They didn't speak for several days, then agreed to avoid the subject.

Milcho told her he was a writer. She asked what he'd published, and he said nothing yet, but he would. Being a writer was a frame of mind. He watched, he observed, he planned stories in his head. She harrumphed. As soon as he got a regular job and a flat, official status, all of that, then he would start; for now, he wrote in his head. She carried on picking, her slender fingers fast and delicate amongst the strawberries. The work ended and she went to Germany while Milcho and the others headed for London. He thought of her for a few days after that. She had a mouth like Krasi's.

'The important thing,' Milcho's literature teacher used to say, 'is to keep your eyes open, see things. A writer is different, set apart from the rest of society.' He looked up at the black and white prints of Botev and Pushkin on the classroom wall. 'Writers are the unnoticed law-makers of society,' he explained another time, and it made the seventeen year-old Milcho feel good. His writing would change the world, he would write the great novel of the new Bulgaria as it emerged from communism and all the other yokes it had endured.

Milcho had phoned Baba at the weekend. She cried, asked when he would start sending the money. That was a brick in his chest. As soon as he had paid off the debt, he'd said. 'What for?' she asked, thinking he spent it on women, so he told her. For the 'special passport' he had needed to get into England. He didn't say how long it would take. There was muffled noise as she handed the phone over to his Dad who asked what he was doing now. 'Working on building sites, it's good money,' Milcho said. He told him how much; more in an hour than his Dad got in several days, an exchange rate that meant nothing really, for everything else cost several days' money too, but he was impressed. There was a pause, then his Dad said, 'A writer on a building site. Like old times, playwrights cleaning windows.' Milcho could hear him chuckling, pleased with himself, but it was OK, he was just being clever. Then the phone was back to Baba; she had something to say. There was a fumbling silence as she steadied the receiver against her ear, Milcho had seen her do it a thousand times, and for a moment he smelt the hills above Sliven in the spring. 'You don't need a special passport, we're in Europe now,' she declared. Milcho said it was complicated, not to worry about it, he would start to send money soon. Then they were saying goodbyes, but they said them simultaneously, neither sure if the other had heard, again, and then again, and still it didn't feel enough to end the call.

'Write what you know,' the teacher said and handed back Milcho's stories about the outlaws. There were no haiduti any more, running through the forests, fighting the devil. Milcho was not sure that there was even a devil now either, though some gaffers came close. There was not much he knew here, he was in a perpetual state of unknowing, looking to Dimiter or Christo all the time. They got up, they worked, they went home, and the cash paid the rent and a little of the debt, a bit left over for everything else. Meanwhile, he wrote in his head: Christo farted like a trumpet; Dimiter snored like the tide; her slender fingers worked fast and delicately. A brick in his heart.

There was something else. He'd asked Baba about Krasi, had they heard anything?

'Who?' She hardly remembered her, so many had left: 'That little thing. She left three years ago, no word. Her mother sits crying all the time.'

'She'll be OK,' Milcho said.

'Cries all the time, stupid woman.'

'I mean Krasi, she'll be OK; not just a pretty face.'

But Baba hadn't heard, she was telling something about the First of March, did they celebrate it, as if he was already English. No, he told her, it was no big deal here.

***

A van careered round the corner and pulled up beside the first cluster of men. The driver only needed three, so he took the Poles who had been there first. When the van had gone, they settled back into their thoughts for a little more until a truck hauled itself into the street and juddered to a halt, exhausted. Dimiter knew the driver, he'd worked for them before. They needed ten, a building site somewhere in south London. They nodded to each other and climbed in the back. Dimiter said they were tough on that site, really tough, and you couldn't be sure you'd be paid either.

That evening the internet café stank of sweat; it was the types you got in there, thought Milcho. The girl indicated a computer without looking at him. The world on the screen was as brightly lit as ever, and he spent half an hour chatting to Bulgarians elsewhere in England, another in Canada, one in New Zealand. It was going well for all of them, they all said so.

'Have you tried this site?' said Christo beside him. Milcho hadn't seen him come in. He looked round the dividing panel at Christo's screen and there was a girl in bra and panties sitting on her bed, typing into a keyboard, then looking up at a screen off camera. The connection wasn't great, the picture froze, then jumped to the girl on all fours, waving her arse in the air. Milcho scowled and went back to his chat. After a bit, Christo groaned, wanting him to look at his screen again. There was a black girl lying across a bed, touching herself through her knickers. Milcho was bored of chatting so he called up the same site. There were 326 girls on-line.

'Click on any, it's free. You can chat, but if you want them to do much, you go private and that costs,' Christo said, then added, 'Check out LizzieCum.'

He was struck by the eerie intimacy, normal girls, some pretty, some not, some on their beds or a sofa in their home, in front of a curtain hiding who knew what, some giggling and flirting, some with the bored weariness of cheap professionals. One girl in a little tartan skirt and white underwear lay back and jiggled her foot in the air for several minutes. There was a teddy bear on the pillow behind her head. Another click, this time to JuicySuck, a worried looking Asian girl with a painfully slow connection. Another click and a blonde girl in what looked like an archetypal eastern block flat, those familiar wall units behind her. She ran her hands across her breasts before returning to the keyboard. The slower connections were irritating so he began to click on new girls quickly: Daisy_squirt, melanieX, blackgoddess, titlicker, GenieSuck, and fairly soon he was thinking of heading back to the house, hotAsiababy, !cum-to-me, wetlips, schoolgirlxx, and maybe watch the TV with Dimiter and the others, ParisDiva, wetSlut, screwmimi, when a look caught his attention just as he clicked again, so he was already on to the next girl before it had registered in his head. He tried to go back, but that didn't work. He hadn't seen the name. It was hardly a thought at this stage, he didn't frame it into words.

Christo scraped his chair back and clapped him on the shoulder, said he'd see him back at the house, then chuckled when he saw Milcho's rapt attention. Milcho nodded in reply as he searched through the names and the small thumbnail photos of tits and arses and astonished expressions, clicking on one after another, titlicker, hornyGirrl, Squirtdani, wetSlut, each one doing what she had been doing before, JuicySuck, melanieX, blackgoddess, until there again, at last, was Krasi. It wasn't so much her mouth; it was the mundane, familiar way in which she had peered at the screen below, frowning a little to read what a punter had said. She flashed a look up at the camera and blew a kiss, then typed at the keyboard. Guest24 had written something Milcho couldn't understand and ItaliSexBomb replied 'all for you in prvt' in yellow print. Then guest87 asked if she was shaved, guest35 said he was coming, guest20 said 'heh, yor pretty!' and ItaliSexbomb replied 'grazia!' and flashed a smile at the camera. She looked thinner in the black bra she was wearing, her shoulders a little hunched. She sat on a bed with a blue curtain behind. For a moment she spoke to someone out of sight, then sniffed disdainfully and returned to the keyboard.

When he left, Milcho had two hours to pay. The bored girl on the desk took the tenner and returned the change without looking at him. He walked back to the house, his body aching from the work that day. They had pushed them hard, but the gaffer hadn't been unhappy and it looked like there was work for the rest of the week. Milcho hadn't written anything to her, he had just watched, recognising the little facial mannerisms that he had grown up with, the way she pushed back her hair, the way she frowned when concentrating. Then the screen blanked out and a message said that she had gone private with someone, which was when he got up to leave. Back at the house, Christo and Dimiter had already turned in so he just nodded to the others and went straight up. Dimiter was already snoring. Milcho lay in the dark and thought about Krasi, and then stopped and thought about writing stories instead. He had this image of the gaffer at work, shouting angrily at the men, and for a moment he would notice that three of the workers each had a small piece of red and white string tied round his wrist. Milcho wasn't sure what he'd do with this idea, but he liked it. He'd use it one day.

Joyriders

Sarah Oswald

I'd been following my brother's trail for two weeks now, and I knew I was close. I never let on to them that I knew, Mum and Pete or the coppers and social services. They had no idea what he was into. But I found out, I figured it all out. He told me, see. Left me clues.

***

I saw him just before he went. It was in the afternoon, after school. I was walking up the grass bank beside the all-night garage. This girl Emma that my brother used to go out with worked there; if there was no-one in the shop she'd let me buy a bottle.

He looked up when I called him, but just nodded and carried on walking.

'Steff! What you doing?'

He stopped and let me catch up, but he was acting as though he had somewhere important to be and he needed to get there badly.

'What's up, butt? What you doing?' I asked him again.

He shuffled his feet. Steff's got really deep blue eyes, like mine, and the same stupid curly hair that grows out like a seventies afro, except his is longer and he never washes it so the grease kind of makes it lie flatter. He looked at me through his fringe, then along the road, then back at me again, back and forth like that a few times.

'Nothing. Where you going?' he said.

'Down the Tunnel.' I dropped my voice. 'You going for a ride?'

He stared straight at me. His pupils were just little dots. I knew he was on one.

'Oh, take us with you!'

He shook his head and grinned, a big grin that pulled his lips back so that his teeth were showing. 'Can't do it, little bro. This one's going be such a mad one!'

He started laughing. He's got this laugh; he pushes his tongue through the gap in his front teeth and makes a sound like steam coming out of a pressure cooker.

'I got to go,' he said, and ran off across the forecourt.

I should have gone with him.

***

I never got to see the body. I went with mum to the morgue but they wouldn't let me see him. When they said I had to wait I got angry and kicked a few chairs around: nothing, really. Mum started yelling and telling the doctors they should lock me up.

They made me sit at end of this corridor while they took mum off to see whether the body they'd found was my brother. They were gone for ages. How long does it take to say, 'yeah that's my son?' or, 'no, that's not him', for fuck's sake?

The woman behind the desk near the seats was ignoring me, filling in some forms. There was a clear plastic bag in front of her on the desk. It had an iPod in it and a keychain thing like the one Steff wore on his belt.

I went over and leant on the desk. She was like those women who come round from social services, with their smart clothes and posh accents. She spoke to me the same way they do too, like they know you've got to do whatever they say because everyone's on their side and you're just nothing. I hate them.

'Can I help you?' she said.

'Is that my brother's stuff?'

'We can't release it until they've identified the body.'

I folded my arms and rested my head on them so that my eyes were level with the bag.

'It is his, I recognise it.'

'It has to be signed for by his next of kin.'

'I'm his brother.'

'Do you have ID?'

I could tell she was getting agitated. I grinned at her and leaned forward, pushing my hair back from my face.

'I look like him, see? Why don't you go down the freezer and check?'

She flinched and stepped back, far enough for me to reach over and grab the bag. She went to snatch it off me but I was already gone, down the corridor and out through the doors.

When I got in I went straight upstairs to Steff's room and got the big chair with all his clothes on it and pushed it in front of the door.

From Steff's window you can see all the houses in our town: rows of miner's cottages all exactly the same, streaming down the hill like veins feeding into the massive main artery of the A470 at the bottom. At school they told us there was a canal there once, before the road. A stem that carried the flow of coal and iron from the roots of Merthyr down toward the sea, so that the city could flower at the other end. The city that sucked the Valleys dry, drained the life from us, grew fat and overblown with its money and its big ideas. Now it sits there all full of itself, and doesn't like to think about the ugly ball of roots and shit that fed it.

The room smelt of fags and cider and sweat. I wanted to hear the last music he'd listened to, but the iPod had melted. It stank of burnt plastic.

His computer was still on. I went over to it, thinking I'd play the last track on his music player instead. I moved the mouse and the screen blinked. He had a photo of this mad graffiti from the Tunnel as his desktop, some bloke called Ogoun. His work was all down the Valley. You'd be driving down the A470 and see his tag in purple and orange on some bridge and think, how the fuck did he get up there? Total commitment.

I hit play. It was some Dub-Step Grime mix; hypnotic, echoing beats. I turned it up, stretched out on the bed, and went through the rest of the bag. There wasn't much besides the iPod and the chain. A silver Zippo lighter, some loose change, and the remains of a pen, melted like the iPod except for the metal bit at the end. That was all. Where was his mobile? His wallet? How did they know it was him?

It was wrong. He'd nicked more cars, better cars, than anyone, and he'd driven them the fastest, and he never crashed and he never got done. They knew it was him, but they couldn't ever catch him at it. Down the Tunnel or over behind the railway line, all the gangs knew about my brother, they all wanted to hang out with him and go riding with him, they all talked about the shit he got up to. When I was at school everyone gave me respect because they knew Steffan was my brother. He was a legend. He would't have just fucked up.

I was thinking all this stuff, about how it might have been Baz or Gareth or anyone in that car, and that loads of people have Zippos and iPods, and even if they were his maybe he'd just dropped them getting out of the car, and he might be wandering around in shock somewhere right now, when the computer made a noise and a reminder popped up on the screen.

Steff must have set for himself before he went out, days before.

'Check the Christmas Special.'

That was all it said.

All kinds of thoughts started rushing into my head at once. I knew he never went out to kill himself, like people were saying, but I also knew from the way he'd looked that day that he was on a bender. Either way, he was never going to be here today to get that message.

So I knew then, that he must have left it for me.

***

'The Christmas Special' was our secret name for the time Steff took me out riding with him, last Christmas. Mum and Pete were pissed up round at Pete's sister's. We were in Steff's room drinking and listening to the radio. I'm not meant to drink, but I do it anyway. Sometimes it makes things seem really clear. 'Lucid', they call it. That's what that night was like. Lucid.

The DJ came on and said, 'You're listening to the Christmas Special,' and Steff jumped off the bed and started pulling on his hoodie.

'Christmas Special!' he said. 'Come on little bro, we'll have our own Christmas fucking Special!'

Christmas is the best day of the year for riding, Steff reckons. Everyone's pissed up in front of the telly, too full to move and go look out the window. Sometimes they even forget to lock up and set their alarms.

We started on the estate, took an old Golf down the dual carriageway at 95, tripping all the cameras. We dumped it on the east side of the city near these new houses and found a Mazda injection. Steff let me drive it all the way down to the Bay.

It was brilliant, just me and him. He showed me how to do handbrake turns in a car park by the posh flats. Then we took a Honda Civic and did a dash through the city, running all the lights because there was fuck all traffic. We heard sirens as we went past the castle and Steff was on one, turning left and right through the back roads behind the University and losing them amongst the student houses

We sat tight for half an hour, swigging White Lightning on a footbridge over the railway line. From up there you could see all the big houses, the ones with bay windows and gardens with gates and hedges. There were fairy lights in all the windows, blinking on and off. Steff caught sight of something over by the houses and started laughing.

'What? What?' I said.

He ran along the bridge and dropped the bottle over the side. It hit the track with a pop.

'Enough of that shit,' he said. 'We got to be pure for this one.'

I followed him down the steps, running to keep up.

He stopped at the end of the street and crouched down beside a garden wall, shushing me up when I got there.

Then I saw it.

A shiny black BMW.

Steff was trying not to laugh out loud. He made a thin, squeaky noise instead, like his pressure cooker had too much water in it. It freaked me out because it didn't sound like him at all.

He was over by the car window before I'd even finished saying, 'No way.'

There was a dull cracking noise. I gritted my teeth, waiting for the alarm to go off, getting ready to run. But the next thing I heard was the engine starting.

I just stood there, like an idiot. Lights came on in an upstairs window.

Steff opened the driver door and shouted, 'What you doing? Get in the car!'

I saw a face at the window. An older bloke with grey hair. Fat. He looked confused, craning his neck to see over the hedge into the street.

Steff revved the engine hard.

'Leon! Get in the fucking car!'

The bloke's eyes widened. His mouth made an angry shape behind the glass.

I ran down the street and caught the rear passenger door, jumping in just as Steff let her go. The g-force threw me back against the seat as we screamed down the road, leaving the stink of burnt rubber behind us.

I thought Steff would be tamping, but as soon as I shut the door he started whooping like a madman, shouting out of the window,

'You're next, you fat bastard!'

He cut the corner and we went almost sideways out of the street, me slamming across the back seat.

'Whoo-Hoo! All right!' he laughed. I caught his eye in the rear view mirror as I sat up and for second I thought he was someone else.

Then he turned round and he looked like Steffan again.

'Get up here, little bro! Look at this - half a tank!'

I clambered into the front as Steff gunned it through the empty streets, holding on tight as we flew past deserted schools and shops and zebra crossings, their yellow lights blinking like the fairy lights, all blurring into one. I had no idea where we were. My head was swimming. I shouldn't drink, really.

'Where we going?'

'Somewhere special! No shit! Christmas fucking special!' he laughed.

We hit the A470 and drove up the Valley at well over a hundred. We turned off on an access road near Trefynan and followed a track up to the pylons. On the other side was a steep bank down into some forestry.

We jumped out at the end of the track and the car went over. For a moment it carried on straight, as if someone was still driving it, then the front end caught on something and stopped moving but the back end carried on, and as we watched the whole car flipped over and the boot hit the ground. There was a noise that reminded me of the time mum pulled out the cutlery drawer too fast and the whole lot smashed down on the kitchen floor. The car tumbled down the bank on its side, crumpling in on itself, until it hit the fence at the bottom and came to rest, amazingly, the right way up.

The noise carried on ringing in the air for a second.

'Is it going to blow?' I asked.

Steff muttered something behind me.

When I looked round he was on his knees at the edge of the bank, whispering under his breath, the same thing over and over but I couldn't hear the words. I could see the whites of his eyes in the dark. I thought something had happened to him, like he was having some kind of fit.

'Steff?'

He stopped and blinked up at me. He looked exhausted, like he'd just had an orgasm or something.

'Christmas fucking special,' he grinned.

***

I knew I wouldn't be able to get down to the Christmas Special from the top of the hill, so I caught the train into Trefynan and walked up through the forestry instead.

The forestry track ran out after a bit so I had to fight my way up through the rows of mouldy pine trees. My trainers got soaked. At the top the trees just end and there's a big chain-link fence with rubbish all along the bottom. After that there's just bare rocks and grass.

Nothing grows up here, except pylons. I hate them. They're all over the Valley, rows of them, steel versions of the forestry. Who gets to decide where they put them, anyway? I don't remember seeing any fucking pylons in Cardiff.

I started walking along the fence toward them, keeping my eye open for a way through.

There was a pit in Trefynan, before. Our grandad would have known where. He reckoned the tops of the hills round here aren't the real tops, just slag from the pits piled up. That's why they have to have the fences; in case it all slides down, like in Aberfan.

It was windy up there and the wires were making that sound, as if something's coming to get you. When I was a kid Steff used to tell me the pylons sucked up the souls of all the people buried in the valley, and that's what electricity was made of, and the humming in the wires was their ghosts screaming. I knew that was bollocks, but it still freaked me out sometimes.

The car was exactly where we'd left it, jammed up against the fence. They'd never get a recovery truck up there. I needn't have worried about getting through either; someone had been there before me and made a big gap underneath the fence, a few metres from the car.

It had been well stripped. The hub caps were gone, tyres, wing mirrors, everything. Brambles had started growing around the wheels. There were empty bottles lying all around. White Lightning.

The car was facing away from me. All the windows were smashed in so I could see there was no-one in it, so I don't know why I slowed down, walking as if I was coming in late and trying to creep past the living room door without mum and Pete seeing. The wires were moaning over my head. Something moved in the driver's seat.

I went really cold, as though my heart was pumping waves of coldness through me. I stopped about a metre from the back of the car and waited. It was like, I could *feel* him.

'Steff?' I said.

Something moved again. There was a noise, like someone clapping, very quietly.

'Steff!'

I ran forward. The headrest had been slashed and a bit of the cover was flapping in the wind, was all. There was no-one there.

I was standing there, feeling stupid, when I noticed the big splash of orange and purple sprayed on the bonnet.

'OGOUN'.

I stared at it.

'OGOUN'.

I sat in the driver's seat and closed my eyes.

My brother was Ogoun.

He had sat here, right here. If I concentrated I could remember exactly what he was wearing that night, remember the smell of that Lynx spray he used mixed with the smell of cider and petrol; I could hear him laughing. If I shut my eyes, I could *be* him, at the wheel, slamming through Cardiff and up the A470, one hundred miles an hour, yelling,

'Christmas fucking special!' and, 'Leon! Get in the fucking car!'

Where was he?

Was that his ghost in the wires?

When I opened my eyes I had my hands out in front of me, where the missing steering wheel should be. I don't know why but I looked around to see if anyone was watching, even though I knew there was nobody up there. But it felt like someone might be there, behind the trees. Watching.

I was shaking. I went to light a fag and dropped Steff's lighter on the floor. I put my hand under the seat to get it, and that was when I found the map.

It was a street map of Cardiff and the Valleys, dog-eared and damp. Older than the car.

Every page had little crosses on it, marked in red pen. I found the place where we'd nicked the Christmas Special. There was a red cross right on the spot where it had been parked. There were others, all over Cardiff, up the valley and into Merthyr. The Graig. Bryn Bach. Stafford Road. Places I didn't know. Some had question marks beside them, as if he couldn't remember exactly and was just guessing. There was a cross by an empty bit of the map down in Cardiff Bay, not built when the map was printed, that might have been the car park where we'd found the Honda.

***

It was dark by the time I got back to Trefynan, and it had started raining. There's not a proper station there, just a metal shelter on a platform that stinks of piss, with a bench that's not quite wide enough to sit on.

There was hardly anyone on the train. I sat by myself at the front of the carriage. The only sound was the train on the tracks and the hum of the lights, and it made me feel sleepy.

I got the map out and looked through it again. It couldn't be just places he'd taken cars from. There weren't any crosses on the estate, for a start, but there were ones in other places that didn't make sense, like the airport. I was trying to figure it out and I think I must have nodded off for a minute, because I started when the train braked for the signals outside town.

The train always stops on the line before our station because there's only one track and they have to wait in case there's a train coming the other way. Sometimes it sits there for ages, but other times it catches you out. No-one really uses our station after dark, so the driver doesn't bother to wait there long; he can be past the platform before you've had a chance to get up and hit the button for the doors to open, so you need to be stood by them, ready.

I must have stood there loads of times, waiting by the doors for the train to start up again and pull into the station, staring out at the grey signal box and the fencing around it, the gravel on the cutting, the backs of the houses that overlooked the tracks.

But it all looked different in the dark. The pale signal box floated in the black space beyond the train, and when I looked up and saw the purple and orange graffiti glowing on its surface something happened: I was back in the moment when I had first seen it, a night I'd completely forgotten, and it was like everything I thought had happened in my life, all the time I'd lived since then, had just been a dream I'd had while I was nodding off on the train.

It was on a Saturday.

Steff had been missing for days, so I nicked some money out of mum's bag and caught the train into Ponty to go look for him.

I found him in the park with his mates. They were sat in the empty paddling pool, drinking cider and taking turns on Baz's skateboard. I showed Steff the money and we went into town and had a couple more bottles. I'm not sure what we did after. I remember being sick on the pavement near the market, then it was dark and we were at the train station. Steff was trying to get me on the train and I was sitting on the floor yelling that I felt bad, and he had to carry me onto the train and everyone was staring.

By the time we stopped at the signals I was dizzy and sweating. Steff got me up by the doors, and that was when I saw the fresh graffiti on the signal box, three metres up a metal pole that was surrounded by barbed wire on the steep-sided cutting.

'OGOUN'.

'Fuck, look at that!' I pointed.

'Pretty cool, eh?' said Steff.

'Fearsome! How do you reckon he does it?'

'He's Ogoun.'

A train rushed past in the other direction, so close that I stepped backwards and lost my balance. Steff caught me, and I was stood right in the same place by the doors in the dark with Steff's arm around my shoulders, and I could feel him standing next to me, whispering slurred words that I'd barely been able to hear over the throbbing of the engine and the ringing in my ears, except this time I heard him fine:

'Ogoun, little bro. Spirit of War, of blood and fire and metal, the High fucking Voodoo Priest of the Valleys. Ogoun's going to bring back the power, take it back from all these poncy fuckers. You'll see. Ogoun's going jump on their backs and ride them like bitches. You wait. Ogoun's the Horseman. Divine fucking Horseman!'

Then the train started up and threw us forward and I had to fight hard not to be sick again so I missed the rest of what he said, and anyway I thought he was just rambling. He did that a lot. People were always saying that Steff was on drugs, sometimes even to my face, but they were wrong.

***

Working out the rest was simple. I went home and checked Steff's computer and found *Divine Horsemen* on his 'favourites'. When it asked for a password I knew it would be 'Ogoun'.

The screen went mad, this crazy mess of colours flickering on and off with a soundtrack like a car crash, and I thought I must have done something terminal to the computer and was telling myself how stupid I'd been when a new window opened with his tag at the top and a pattern of red lines at the bottom. In the middle was this:

> "A MESSAGE FROM OGOUN
>
> It's easy. A rock in a sock to the passenger window and you're in. Don't do the driver window or you'll get soaked if it rains. Little hatchbacks are the best, Fiestas and Astras, girly cars. It's best at night, down some residential street just off the city centre. Police too busy in town, everyone who has to get up for work all gone to bed. Quiet. Sirens in the distance but they're not coming for you. Not yet.
>
> Just before I do a car I get this taste in my mouth, as though it's full of blood, a gum-rush like when you're coming up on speed. When the window cracks and all those perfect little squares of glass fall blue-green at my feet my head starts to spin and I know the spirit of Ogoun is coming in. If I hesitate, if I lose it - then he knows it's not good enough. That's when the crook-lock jams or the cover won't come off the steering column, or I hear someone coming and I panic.
>
> But if I don't bottle out, if I jump in totally bold, then he'll take it from there and everything will go smoothly. Put my hood up and keep my head low and I'm not even there; if you passed by now all you'd see is an empty space between the front and rear windscreens, everything as it's supposed to be. You wouldn't see me rip off the crook-lock and wire her up. I don't even have any thoughts in my head

then, I've given it up to Ogoun and it's him making my hands work, feeling the pulse of the city and making the spark between the wires, that beautiful moment when it all comes to life then quick, quick, pump the gas and whop it into gear and by the time you see my head above the wheel you're too late, we're already gone, Ogoun and me screaming down your road and out into the streets.

I'm going to waste this city. I'm going to take everything, trash it and burn it and fuck it all up. Just you wait. I'm coming.

OGOUN."

It was all here, on this site. It explained everything. The pattern is a Vever. At the top is our world, at the bottom is theirs. You draw the Vever on the ground to invoke the spirit. You draw it in petrol and burning rubber. You make a sacrifice to give him energy. The spirit enters through the centre post, the axis. The A470. The spirits are your ancestors. They take possession of you, your body is the vehicle that lets them loose in this world.

Ogoun is the spirit of war. Of blood, fire, and metal.

I understand everything now.

I joined up the crosses on Steff's map to make Ogoun's Vever. There's a bit missing right at the top. Up above Merthyr, in the mountains.

So now I know where he went. And I know that he didn't die in that car, because even if it was his body, he is Ogoun, the spirit. All I have to do is find the right sacrifice and finish the Vever. Finish what he started and bring him back. I'll be the vehicle.

And I'm writing all this here so that you'll know, when all the shit goes down and the Power rises in the Valleys, you'll know it was me that did it, that I brought him back: my brother, Ogoun.

***

I never meant to be gone for that long. When I saw Leon that day at the garage it was the worst I'd ever been. I was so fucked up when I went in to see Emma that she thought I was going to kill myself. She made her sister's boyfriend come and get me and they basically locked me up in their flat until I came down, and kept it all quiet to stop anyone from coming round and slipping me something while they were out.

The bloke in the car turned out to be some boy racer who'd got trolleyed one night and lost it coming down Caerphilly Mountain. By the time they'd figured out it wasn't me, Leon had already gone missing.

The old bill have been round loads of times but the stupid bastards never checked the computer. I found Leon's blog on Divine Horsemen just by looking back on the history. I'd forgotten that was where I'd got the idea for the whole 'Ogoun' thing. I don't know who wrote the original blog; I just nicked the design. I don't remember reading any of that voodoo stuff.

I never realised how much he looked up to me. He must have been the only person in the world who thought I was cool. How was I to know he would try to copy me? I swear, I never said any of that shit to him on the train. And I don't know where he got that map from, if there even was a map. I'd been up to that wreck loads of times and I never found any map under the seat. But that's Leon, see: he's not right. Not right in the head.

I'm not going to tell anyone, not until I find him.

I have to find him. It's all my fault, see.

There's only so many places he could have gone. I bought myself a map like his and I've been up there every chance I've had, looking, crossing off all the places I've checked.

It'll be somewhere up high, where you can see the whole Valley. Above all the houses, and roads, and pylons. And when I find him I'll tell him I'm sorry.

North Cold

Tania Hershman

Global warming can be intangible, but melting ice: that we can see.
New Scientist magazine, 27 August 2005

There is a small town in the north that is cold all year round. The people living in the town have come to accept it as they accept that the sun rises, sets and rises again. Cold is the natural order of things. No-one talks about the weather except visitors, who do not stay for longer than they must.

The people of the town have fashioned their own measures against the cold, although *against* is not the correct word, for they do not view it as an enemy. They never leave their houses without several layers of clothing. They wear a hat to bed and sleep under several blankets. Not many babies are born in this town. Cold is effective at dampening even the most burning ardour.

The people of this town have thicker skin than most; here, people live further inside themselves.

So it was that on a Thursday in January a young man arrived. He descended from the bus, which made its journey from the south once daily, and rubbed his hands together.

'My, my,' he said to no-one in particular, 'They were certainly right about this,' and he blew on his hands, whose bareness was already attracting stares from the people passing. No-one said anything. What should they say? 'Wrap up warm, son, you'll catch your death?' The people of the town were not so forthright. They preferred to be left to their business and not to poke into the business of others. 'What comes will come, to one and all,' could have been the town's motto.

The young man looked around him with a great curiosity. Then he picked up his large bag from the frozen ground, slung it over his shoulder, and began to walk with purpose into the centre of the town as if it were not completely foreign to him. The young man, whose name was Seargent, possessed a confidence that everything he needed he would find, and so he strode on, never thinking of asking for directions to the hotel.

This being a small town, the hotel was where expected: on the main street.

'I would like a room,' Seargent said to the man at the desk, setting his bag down beside him.

The older man looked at the younger, who was wearing only a thin jacket, no hat or scarf, and whose face was the pink of those who have only just arrived and still describe the weather as *exhilarating*. The man nodded slowly, for no one made quick movements in this town, turned around and fetched a key from the board behind.

'Twenty-nine,' he said. 'Up the stairs, first left, first right. Towels in the bathroom, breakfast's extra.'

'Okay,' said Seargent, taking the key and his bag. He headed for the stairs, whistling as he went. The man behind the counter watched him, wincing slightly at the whistle. Seargent felt the man's eyes on his back. *That's right*, the young man thought, *that's right*.

In truth, Seargent was not as young as he appeared. He had a method for preserving his youthful appearance which he was not planning on divulging, even to his fiancée, Elaine, whom he planned to marry the following June. This secret had been handed down to him by an elderly aunt who favoured him over her twelve other nephews and nieces. Calling him aside during a family occasion when he had only just entered into the age at which boys' faces harden and bristle, she passed the knowledge to him as it had been passed to her by her grandmother. After she had told it, she moved closer to the boy. 'You will not live longer,' she warned, 'but you will appear to be twenty years less than you are.' Looking herself not a day past forty, though she had in fact overtaken sixty last birthday, she took hold of his shoulders. 'This can be both blessing and curse, you understand me?' Seargent, who didn't, just nodded. He saw only the blessing, and his aunt saw that he would fall because of it and she could do nothing to prevent the fall.

The boy kissed his aunt on the cheek, and if he noticed that her skin was icy despite the late August heat, the thought passed straight through and out of his mind. With her aged eyes, that told anyone who looked closely at her smooth, soft face that mischief was at work here, his aunt watched him run back to his cousins and sighed for what was to come.

In the hotel room, Seargent shut the curtains and unpacked his bag, hanging up two dark suits in the wardrobe and placing the large metal box under the single bed. Then he sat down in the chair and smiled a smile that a room so small, dark and musty rarely saw. He would soon find out if all the years of preparation had come to something, or to nothing. He would soon know if he would make his fortune.

Struck with a sudden hunger, he stood, put on his jacket, and went to discover what the town could offer. He ran down the stairs, whistling as he jogged through the lobby.

The man at the hotel desk watched, annoyed.

'Who is he?' he asked the chambermaid who had come to request the next day off work due to her father's worsening overnight.

'Don't know,' said the chambermaid, whose father's condition had not changed but whose boyfriend demanded she come out with him to the woods. Because she was more afraid of her boyfriend than of losing her job, she was doing what she had to do.

'No word of how long he's staying, no idea at all,' mumbled the man.

'That's all right then?' asked the chambermaid.

'Go on with you,' the old man said, and slowly bent to reach the employee book on the lower shelf and log the change.

***

The next morning, Seargent rose late. The sun was already high in the sky, although the town did not feel it. Seargent smelled the air and nodded. He washed and dressed quickly and then withdrew the case from underneath the bed. From the case he took a large ball, the size of a small watermelon, but not so heavy that he could not hold it comfortably in both hands. The ball was made of metal, silver in one light, golden in another, and despite the dullness of the day, it shone. It was an object that held your gaze, letting you look at nothing else.

Seargant stood by the window. Setting the ball on the sill, he opened the window wide and the cold air flowed in. He picked up the globe which had begun to tremble.

'That's right,' he said, 'that's right,' and, holding it on the boundary between inside and out, he closed his eyes and breathed a deep breath.

A substance began to stream from the sides of the ball, yellow in colour and with a texture like steam. It flowed out and down, towards the town and over the town, until the whole area was covered in a fine buttercup mist.

***

In the woods, the chambermaid's boyfriend was fumbling with the fifth layer of her woollens while she lay there, her head on frozen leaves, next to her the hat that had fallen off as he manhandled her. She felt nothing. She stared at the frost-covered tree stump beside her. Her boyfriend grunted as he made progress, and inside herself the chambermaid sighed. She could not even cry, because she knew that her tears would freeze as they ran down.

Something stroked her cheek and she started. *He* was still down the other end engaged in exploratory digging. There was no-one there. But her cheek was warm. Slowly she realized that it was not just her face - her body started to experience a sensation she had never had outside of her heavily-blanketed bed.

She was hot.

She sat up.

'Stop!' she said. 'Can't you feel it!' He grunted but broke off from what he was doing to stare at her. The chambermaid struggled to her feet and began pulling off her clothes. 'I'm hot! I'm hot!' she cried. She threw the clothes at her boyfriend, who fell backwards under the weight of the wool, and the chambermaid, wearing only her underwear, started running towards the town.

***

Seargent walked out into the street. The townspeople were converging, wanting to know what it was, this strange new sensation. People were disrobing, large jumpers and cardigans, socks and thick tweed trousers lying on the ground.

'Boiling!'

'Something's not right, I'm ...'

'Have to take these off, it's...'

'Never in all my days, have I...'

'Praise be....'

...*to me*, thought Seargent. *Praise be to me*, and he stepped into the middle of Main Street and started walking through the crowds.

No-one knew what was happening, why the cold was leaving their frozen town, but one man had an idea. Wearing only his vest and underpants, he left the hotel desk unattended, took his master key and made his way slowly upstairs, unfamiliar sweat gathering on his forehead.

It took him a few minutes to find the ball, which was back in its case under the desk. Holding it in both hands, he felt coursing through him the heat from a thousand warm souls, the breath of a thousand people living their days in the sun in every country Seargent had travelled to. The old man's lips, so long frozen into an expression of disdain, began to turn upwards. Inside him ice was shifting. He walked towards the open window and held the ball outwards.

'See!' he cried, but his voice was weak and no-one heard him, just as they did not see the yellow streaming again over their town.

Seargent saw.

Seargent saw that there was more where it should have stopped, more when there was already plenty.

'No!' he cried, but he was too far away. He began running towards the hotel but the heat was inside him and his legs moved more and more slowly. He stopped and sank to his knees. He put his hands to his face and his fingers felt out the wrinkles crawling across his brow. Moving upwards, he found his hair receding away from him. His fingers began to bend and stiffen. Age crept into every muscle, every joint, not just the twenty years that he had pushed deep inside of him, but twenty and twenty and twenty more, for the damage he had done to his nature. His face crumpled into folds of old skin, his vision began to blur, and still the golden haze flowed across the town.

Seargent cried out for help, but no-one heard him. The townspeople, naked now, were dancing in the glow of the warm yellow light, and they danced around him in their joy, whirling and singing, as he sank slowly down towards the ground.

Miss Vandermeyer and the Star Baby

Emma Seaman

Miss Helena Vandermeyer had never entertained any real pretensions to beauty. Even as a young woman with the bloom of youth flushing her cheeks, the dreaded Vandermeyer nose had prevented her ever looking girlish and rosebud-demure, as was then the prevailing fashion. Now somewhere deep into her forties, she favoured outrageous little hats, flamboyant clashing hues and defiantly cropped, Marcel-waved hair which threw her dramatic bone structure into sharp relief. Not even the latest Parisian fashions or all the cosmetic arts of Miss Lauder or Miss Rubenstein could make her beautiful, but she was pleased to sometimes overhear herself remarked upon as striking. She would consider anything, (simply anything my dear!), rather than the horror of being regarded as spinsterishly dried up.

It wasn't, she often reminded herself, as if she hadn't had her opportunities for conventional happiness. She had even been betrothed once; to a somewhat moose-jawed young man, heir to a considerable fortune of his own and therefore deemed suitable in every way. But he had died. She occasionally, a little guiltily, let people assume he had died in the Great War, rather than more prosaically, yet somehow more tragically, in the influenza epidemic that followed. Even after that, though a little too old to be a bright young thing, she had received offers, some quite serious. But Helena was the true daughter and grand-daughter of silver barons, and was no fool; she was acutely aware that the extensive Vandermeyer mines, the prospering tool company, the country estate in Connecticut were all a brighter lure than her rather piercing blue eyes.

Of course, there was a time when she could have legitimately taken her pick of those young (oh far too young!) men with smooth tongues and ever-ready smiles, or the older gents who stole avuncular arms around her waist, secretly itching to get their hands on the Vandermeyer portfolio rather than on her. But a shred of romance ('silliness' her mother would have called it) lodged deep within her, ensuring that she longed to be courted for her self and not her fortune. And so Helena, the last remnant of the Vandermeyer genes, quietly doubled and trebled the money left her and had spent the last ten years following her whim; wintering in the sun, flitting into New York as it suited her, indulging her taste for the latest fashions in Paris and London every Spring and Fall. Hence this ill-fated European trip.

Simply everything about this voyage had been wrong, she thought, swaying gently to the uneasy, queasy motion of the ship. She pressed a handkerchief firmly against her mouth, trying to quell the dreaded mal-de-mer by sheer force of will. Helena was well used to sea-travel, but the Heligoland Bay seemed unusually choppy this evening, and it was bitterly cold out here on the frayed edges of the North Sea. She wished she'd been able to take a route that alighted somewhere clement for a few weeks. But at least this way she'd be back in New York in less than a fortnight, in time for Easter, and could put all this unpleasantness behind her. If the chattering tongues in Berlin were right, then she wouldn't be doing any European travelling for a while. Maybe it was that tense, anticipatory atmosphere in Germany that had affected the passengers. She had never been bothered with political affairs and so the annexation of Austria had been, she conceded somewhat shamefacedly, a surprise. The Germans were triumphal, exhilarated, giddy; and the majority of her fellow voyagers seemed to be less *travelling* and more, well, to put it bluntly, *fleeing*.

While overnighting in Hamburg awaiting a suitable berth, she had made tentative arrangements to meet with a very distant cousin; a diplomat's wife who was travelling back to America with her children. Helena hoped the woman would be too preoccupied with her small ones to batten upon her too much. She didn't want some dowdy mother with brats hanging from her skirts cramping her own modest style and, Lord knows, she needed a little on-board divertissement. Helena duly met this Mrs Cumberbatch briefly on the Promenade deck, hurrying her brood towards their cabin.

Elspeth Cumberbatch motioned gaily to her offspring, introducing them with an encouraging smile to this strikingly-dressed stranger. Gazing at them all, Helena felt a faint horror. It would surely be cramped in a normal cabin with, gosh darn, how many children did that woman have after all? And all girls! There was a tiny one, wobbling proudly but unsteadily on chubby little legs, attached to her mother by leading reins. A second child (Ha! Helena had predicted it!) clung to her mother's rather frumpy skirt, hiding her pink cheeks in its full folds. The eldest held back, gazing owlishly at Helena's rakishly perched toque and wildly fluttering cape. Helena looked back at her sternly; her experience of small children was that they had a propensity for saying something devastating, usually about one's personal appearance.

Mrs Cumberbatch was bustlingly full of opinions about the furore in Germany and the reasons for her hasty departure sans spouse.

'Gerald, my husband, he's in the diplomatic corps and says there will certainly be a storm and we are best off out of it. Men know these things,' she said confidently, 'Well, some things – they're absolutely useless at others. Gerald couldn't tell you what Lottie's favourite toy is, or which particular foodstuffs Martha absolutely won't eat.'

She looked at her litter with pride. Helena failed to look enthusiastic, her mind glazing over at the thought of ten days of baby-talk and interminable infant anecdotes. What was it about having children that made presumably intelligent women become so unutterably dull? She hoped she could mostly avoid her during the journey. Even a lonely week reflecting on the tedious intricacies of European politics would surely be preferable.

Once queasily ensconced in her cabin, Helena surveyed the daunting pile of her luggage, including a steamer trunk (three others were, hopefully, lodged down in the hold), a pile of lavishly beribboned bandboxes (the fruits of her brief stay in London) plus an assortment of small portmanteaux, several handbags and an umbrella. She sighed and rummaged fruitlessly for her sleeping pills, without which, Lord knows, she couldn't sleep a single wink.

As she unlocked her trunk, she caught a slight motion flickering at the very edge of her vision. I'm so very tired of travelling, she thought wearily, pressing the cool back of her hand to her eyes to still them. Then she heard a definite rustle. She looked sternly at the new chintz Gladstone bag she had purchased in London. Was it just the rather busy floral print that gave it the impression of moving? The room swam before her eyes and the bag gave a little lurch, as if propelled from inside. Then a definite bulge appeared in one soft cloth side, as if something were pushing from within. She felt increasingly nauseous. Rats! Something must have gotten into the bag while she waited on the dock. She thought rats were supposed to leave ships, not hitch a lift onboard.

She scuttled across the cabin, desperately reaching for the bell to summon the cabin attendant. Then she stopped herself. By the time someone attended her ringing, the creature would be gone, fled under her bed, to creep out in the night. Helena knew she couldn't rest with a rat in the cabin. The boat was full, there wouldn't be another decent suite available, and besides, the general fuss and botheration of moving was just the sort of thing she couldn't abide. Chin jutting, she snatched up her umbrella; she would just wale away on the bag until the nasty thing was dead. Then she reflected that the bag was absolutely the latest mode and beating an animal to submission within it would almost certainly spoil the bag as well as the contents, which unfortunately included her spectacles, compact, toothbrush and most of her documentation.

Instead, she edged warily across the floor, umbrella held at arm's length. She thrust the crook through the handles of the bag, planning to push it outside the cabin door and (a master stroke, she felt) let the foul beast escape into the corridor. But with the wretched luck she now expected from this trip, the bag was unlatched and fell open as she lifted it. She gasped, stopped stock still, expecting the trapped animal to spring out, teeth bared, and leap for her throat. But nothing happened. She heard a faint cry. Curiosity overcame her and she peered down. What she saw was far more shocking than any sharp-toothed rodent. There was a baby, a real live human baby, nestled down in a crimson and purple paisley silk shawl that she knew wasn't hers. The baby blinked several times, startled by the light now flooding into its hiding-place, then opened its blue eyes, blinked and smiled gummily right up at her. Golly, she thought, and was surprised into smiling back.

She gazed at the baby, her mouth ajar. It wasn't a fat baby, but plump enough to show it had been fed and loved, and though its clothes were rather faded, as if washed many times, they were certainly clean. I wonder what the fashions are for babies this season, she thought giddily, disapproving of the effect of the child's pale skin against that luridly-coloured shawl. She had occasionally bought christening layettes from Macy's, but they were composed of froth and frills and general pinkness. This child was wearing – well what would you call them? Little overalls? They looked to Helena's eye (though certainly no expert in making over and mending) as if they had been cut down and adjusted from the clothing of a much larger child. There was a patch roughly tacked onto the front of the blue stripy coveralls. A yellow star. Sweet, thought Helena, still utterly bemused. The baby scratched at the star reflexively; the heavy material made scraping noises under its tiny fingernails and it seemed to find the texture interesting, the sound curious.

Helena picked up the child and laid it gingerly on her bed. It stretched out its legs joyfully, seeming pleased to be released from the confines of the bag. There was a piece of yellow paper tucked carefully into the folds of the shawl. Helena unfolded the paper; it was cheap and fibrous, the ink spreading on the page. The lettering was awkward, as if by someone unused to writing, at least in English. *Take care of my child please,* she read, *they have already come for my husband and I am afraid of what will happen now. You will find it such a good baby and you look as if you could provide a better life.*

Now that, thought Helena, bending over to peer at the child more closely, is highly ambiguous. Did the writer think I looked kind, or just rich? She knew a sharp spurt of outrage; what did they take her for? A sucker? She felt a movement at her chest and looked down to see the baby clasping her, its hand swirling like a little starfish, opening and closing, seeking something to cling onto. There was a photograph slipped in with the letter, a cheap posed studio shot of a young couple, presumably the child's parents. She wondered if someone could trace the family from the torn little picture. They looked nice enough, the husband holding his bride's arm with a proud smile. The mother was a little plain, but then, Helena thought bitterly, who am I to comment?

The child was grizzling now, making a squeaky, rusty sort of noise. She simply must find someone to deal with this ridiculous situation. But again, as her hand stretched for the bell, she had a sudden clear vision of what would happen if she called the purser, got the captain involved, made this official. What the jiggers would she say?

'Someone appears to have left their child in my room and can you sort it out, there's a good fellow?'

She couldn't even claim it was mistaken luggage – it was her bag alright, and a very distinctive one at that. She moved the child awkwardly to the crook of her other arm, trying to calm that peculiar noise before it escalated into something worse. Holding it in this new position, she realised it was absolutely sodden, soaked through. She shuddered delicately; she'd never had to deal with diapers before but intuited that the strange noise was connected to a degree of discomfort on the child's part.

She sighed; she supposed at least she could dry the child off a little while she decided what the blazes she was going to do. It took her a while to unhook the coveralls and unwrap the bundle of soft wrappings tied around its loins. She peered into the soaking cloth. Oh, it was a boy then. She was pleased to resolve that question. And the napkin was (oh fortune smiled!) just wet, nothing worse. She dampened one of her handkerchiefs in the hand basin, glad that a persistent head-cold had lead her to pack some sensible linen squares as well as her usual lace-edged frivolities.

Once cleaned, and dried with another handkerchief, she wrapped one of her smallest face towels crosswise around his bottom. But what to fasten it with? She contemplated her jewellery roll. There was her grandmother's pearl and ruby brooch, or perhaps that little gold and diamond crescent? Then she settled, commending herself on her common-sense, on a rather starkly modern platinum bar brooch she'd purchased in London. Less ornament for the little one to catch his fingers on and it had a good stout fastening. Even so, it was hard to get the pin through the layers of towel and she prodded gently, afraid of spearing him with the sharp point. After a couple of minutes' wrestling, she stepped back to admire her handiwork.

'That looks rather fine, young man. There aren't many babies who can boast of wearing hundred-guinea diaper pins.'

He seemed to appreciate her efforts, kicking his legs happily in the air. Helena frowned. Even the platinum pin, Asprey's finest, wouldn't stop the towel from eventually slipping off that wriggling round bottom. She sighed, and took out a pair of clean panties, sacrificing one of Maison Clotilde's luxurious silk crepe creations to the good cause. In deference to his sex, she selected a pistachio-green pair, pulled them over the towel and brooch arrangement, and tied the excess fabric in a neat knot on each hip. That should hold it. His coveralls were still a little damp in the bottom area, but there was no alternative, they had to go back on.

Helena sat down on the edge of the bed, still clutching the boy. She suddenly felt very faint. What if she had not been feeling so weary, unusually queasy, and had gone for a stroll, or even for a late dinner? She could have returned to a dead baby, suffocated in her new English handbag. She shuddered at the very thought. How on earth would she have explained that one away? Her head was spinning. This wasn't what she was used to. And the dry wrapper had not stopped his cries; they were escalating in volume and intensity. She felt as if her brain was melting, as if the cries were piercing through her, as if her teeth would be shaken loose from her head.

The desperate, urgent need to stop that wretched noise temporarily outweighed her lifelong desire for privacy. Oh Lord, now he was crying, an actual tear. That simply wasn't fair. Her throat closed and she felt tears springing to her own eyes at the sight of that oily little drop rolling down his cheek. His hands were clenched, body rigid, eyes scrunched up as if in pain. Perhaps he was ill, dying? She couldn't stand the thought. She had to find that woman, Mrs Cumberbatch; she had children, would know what to do. She scooped the baby up, wrapped him in the gaudy shawl and laid him gently into the Gladstone bag. Being back in the dark confines of the bag stilled his crying to an insistent, anguished whimper.

Slipping out of her stateroom, she made her way along to the first class cabin section. She flinched like a criminal when she saw the cabin attendant walking towards her down the corridor, clutching the bag to her chest, holding it open a little so the child could breathe, without letting the attendant see him. Please don't let the kid howl now, she prayed.

Mrs Cumberbatch opened her door at the second knock; there was a faint suggestion of impatience at this evening visit, though her smile was pleasant enough.

'I seem to have acquired a baby,' Helena said plaintively. 'And he won't stop crying.'

Mrs Cumberbatch took a long thoughtful look at Helena's tired eyes, her rumpled clothes, her air of quiet desperation. 'You'd better come in,' she said.

Helena realised she was being watched by three pairs of wide dark eyes, like chipmunks or other small wild creatures. The Cumberbatch girls, in frilly nightdresses, sat on their mother's bed, gazing at her open-mouthed.

Elspeth raised her eyebrows at Helena's unusual mode of baby-transport and gently lifted the boy out of the bag.

'The poor kiddie probably needs milk; that's a hunger cry if ever I heard one. When did he last feed?'

Helena shrugged helplessly.

'Never mind, I'm sure we can spare a bottle and some of our bedtime milk for this little fellow, can't we girls?' She snuggled him close. He howled and thrust his damp, tear-streaked face into the folds of her dressing-gown, seeking milk where there was none. 'Oh dear,' laughed Mrs Cumberbatch, 'there's nothing in there for you.' Helena felt irrationally annoyed, wishing for a moment – what? That she could nurse this baby herself?

There was a tap at the door. The cabin attendant brought in a pannikin of hot water. He was far too well trained to betray any surprise at the sight of so much night-attired femininity. Helena sat down with a thump in the cabin's only armchair. She felt exhausted. Elspeth placed the squalling baby into her arms.

'He obviously trusts you,' she said, 'You'd better have him, he won't settle with me.' Helena held the baby awkwardly, unused to the weight. 'Tuck him well down, there; cradle his head,' Elspeth prompted, handing Helena a hastily poured bottle. Helena slipped the bottle-teat into his mouth, settling him into the crook of her arm. Sucking hungrily, greedily, he quietened as suddenly as if a switch had been flicked. Elspeth smiled comfortably. 'It's like magic isn't it, the way the noise stops when the milk starts to flow?'

She bustled around, chasing the girls into their bunks in the adjoining cabin and admonishing them to go to sleep instantly. But Helena hardly heard them. She looked down at the child as he fed, drowning in those violet-blue eyes looking so trustingly up at her. He seemed to become drowsy, closing his eyes in concentration, taking longer with the milk, his breathing slowing, eyelids heavy.

Elspeth Cumberbatch returned from settling her girls, sat down on the bed and said calmly, 'I think you'd better tell me what's going on.'

It took little time for Helena to explain her acquisition of the baby. She sat quietly holding him, head bowed, as he drained the bottle to the last rattling, wheezy drops. Elspeth was silent for a few moments, looking thoughtfully at them both, then she shook herself and asked, 'Is he wet?'

'I changed him earlier,' replied Helena, faux-casual, proud of her competence.

Elspeth unswaddled him, unwinding the shawl. She gazed at him for a moment, her mouth suddenly twisting. 'Oh poor mite,' she said, 'poor little fellow,' and she picked the baby up and cradled him protectively to her chest.

'What's wrong?' asked Helena, suddenly afraid.

'He's a Jew, Helena.'

'Why should that matter?'

'It means his mother must have loved him very, very much.'

'I don't see how abandoning your child to strangers, however affluent they may be, proves your love.'

Elspeth replied impatiently, 'It's the yellow star. They used to do it in the Middle Ages. I've heard rumours that some of the places Germany has occupied have started it again…

marking out the Jews so they are easier to pick out, or pick off. His mother was playing fair, she wanted you to know what he is.'

'Well, I've heard rumours, of course…' Helena's voice trailed off as she examined her attitude to those whispers of discord. At least the trains ran on time, that's what everyone said, just like with Il Duce in Italy. The Germans had a certain kind of brutal efficiency one could half-admire after being exasperated with the lacksadaisical attitude of certain European countries, the French, for example. And these new Germans had a definite sense of style, she thought guiltily; all that scarlet and black, the grand buildings, the sheer dynamism. Elspeth smiled grimly, as if reading her mind, and pulled a crumpled, much-studied pamphlet from her capacious handbag.

Helena read it swiftly, heartsick at being forced to confront those rumours in ugly black gothic type. It started with harassment, then moved slowly but surely to outright persecution. The pages documented a stealthy erosion of rights and livelihoods and eventually liberty. How awful, how truly shocking. The text was illustrated with grainy newspaper photographs; of children being mocked at school for their racial heritage, University professors stripped of their jobs and forced to sweep the streets, of families being evicted, broken up, forcibly detained. And finally, darker hints of worse, much worse.

'It's all true,' Elspeth said softly, 'Gerald has been trying to raise awareness back home but finds people won't take it seriously; they're all more worried about the Bolshevik threat. Anti-Jewish feeling isn't unique to the Germans, you see.'

Helena held the pamphlet tightly in her hand, crushing the paper as she absorbed this information. She was frequently asked to fundraising lunches for various charitable causes adopted by ladies with time and compassion on their hands, but their donations were always carefully distant; heartbreak at several removes. This was real, happening here and now, and to people like her. The Vandermeyers had been conscientiously attending the New York Episcopalian church for several generations, but Helena was aware that somewhere not very far back her ancestors were almost certainly Jewish.

'I suppose this comes as a shock to you,' said Elspeth soberly. 'Not a lot of Jews in your social circle, I would imagine.'

Helena decided not to let that one pass. 'Many of my friends were originally Jewish; a lot of people are, in the fashion world. Besides, Vandermeyer is not exactly a WASP-y name.'

Elspeth shrugged, her attention back with the baby. She deftly undid his little coveralls, saw Helena's handiwork and smiled. Helena said crossly, 'It's not as if I carry baby wrappers in my luggage, I hadn't anticipated this.'

'Who would?' said Elspeth, 'I never heard the like; well only once.'

'Really?' said Helena, wondering if other cross-continental liner passengers had been caught by the same trick.

'In the Bible,' Elspeth said triumphantly, 'all human life is there. It's as if the Good Lord has sent the child to us.'

Helena rummaged fruitlessly through Sunday-school memories; bible stories had not played a large part in her life of late.

'Moses, of course,' Elspeth said. 'Like Moses, his mother has cast him adrift to begin a new life where he may be safe.' Helena regarded the child on Elspeth's lap. He did look rather dignified in repose, as if he could grow into being a Moses. 'Moses' sister watched to make sure Pharoah's daughter picked up the baby safely,' added Elspeth, who evidently had perfect biblical recall. Helena cast her mind back to the docks, trying to remember seeing anyone watching her. She hadn't noticed anything unusual. The quay at Hamburg had been dark, squally and cold and she'd hurried aboard without a backwards glance.

'It was such a risk to take, anything could have gone wrong,' said Elspeth.

Helena shuddered. You don't know the half of it, she thought, remembering her initial impulse to beat the bag with her umbrella. 'Maybe they slipped a little something into his bottle to keep him quiet,' she offered.

Elspeth looked reflective for a moment, then said softly, 'Or maybe he's just a baby who has had to learn when it is safe to cry.'

She re-wrapped him carefully in the shawl and handed him to Helena.

Helena snorted, 'Not much of a legacy, is it? A cheap silk shawl, a torn photo and a letter consigning him to the care of a complete stranger.'

'That shawl was probably the softest, nicest thing his mother possessed,' said Elspeth thoughtfully. Helena felt like a complete heel. 'You don't have to keep him you know,' Elspeth said slowly, testing the water, 'Gerald always wanted a boy, to carry on the Cumberbatch name.' Helena couldn't think why anyone would want to perpetuate the name of Cumberbatch, but let her continue. 'I can't have any more, so Gerald might be willing to take him on. No-one on board will notice another child; in all the hurry I doubt they counted the little ones on. Janet can share with Lottie; this little fellow can have her crib.'

For one faint-hearted moment, Helena was tempted to fall onto Elspeth Cumberbatch's plump motherly bosom and let her sort it all out. Then she looked down at little Moses' hand, wound into the fabric of her blouse, his damp clutching fingers holding on to her with his tenacious grip. This may seem like a bizarre interlude to me; a shipboard story, a temporary inconvenience, but it's life or death for him, she thought, and I have to step up to the mark. Old Nathaniel Vandermeyer always put his success down to being in the right place at the right time. 'Know when it's your moment; seize the opportunity and don't let it slip through your fingers,' he'd say. She suspected that this was not what he'd had in mind – his granddaughter rescuing an abandoned baby; but maybe this was all she had.

'He's crumpling your lovely blouse,' Elspeth said, breaking into her thoughts and reaching out to gently detach Moses' tiny damp fingers from Helena's raspberry-red silk mousseline confection.

'Oh, I'm not bothered about that,' Helena said impatiently. She straightened her shoulders, stood up. 'His mother left him with me,' she said, 'I can't shuffle him off.' She somehow found she didn't want to relinquish him now, even for a moment. 'A true Vandermeyer shoulders responsibilities. Father always said that's the curse of money.'

Helena had never understood him until this very moment. She had always found being the rich Miss Vandermeyer preferable to any alternative, but now she had a glimmering of what those responsibilities might be. And what that might mean to little Moses, in his future. 'People think I'm eccentric anyway; they may even think I went abroad to find him.' She tested that thought and found she didn't really mind all that much. After all, she was aware that the luxury of money could buy her any amount of help. Elspeth Cumberbatch smiled, head on one side. 'I'm glad for you my dear,' she said obscurely, and left it at that.

Leaving a drowsy Martha in charge of her now-sleeping sisters, Elspeth loaded a bag with bottles, spare wrappers and even some of little Janet's vests, and helped Helena back through the nearly-silent ship to her stateroom. At the door Elspeth surprised them both by hugging the older woman. 'I'll see you both in the morning,' she said, and hurried gratefully back to her girls.

Helena sat for nearly an hour watching Moses sleep in her arms. Eventually he stirred and cried, a thin wail that rapidly became louder, more insistent. Helena rose to ring the bell, to summon the night-steward to bring a can of hot water to heat one of the bottles Elspeth had lent her. After just half of that bottle, Moses' eyes closed again and his mouth opened, slackened in sleep. She laid him down on the bed, busying herself by unpacking a few items she'd need in the morning. After a few minutes she went back to him, touched his face, his hands. He felt chilly, the little hands cold, almost clammy. He was so still.

Panicking, she lay down beside him, tucking him into the curve of her body. Instinct taking over, she nestled his downy head into the crook of her arm, enfolding him in her warmth. He snuffled slightly, whimpering, then settled down into her embrace.

Once she was sure he was asleep again, she reached behind her with one hand, finding the soft shawl and tucking it gently round him, careful not to disturb his sleep. She gazed down at his face, at the spiky dark eyelashes curving against the smooth skin, the uptilted, slightly squashed-looking nose and sleep-flushed, plump round cheeks. He is such a handsome child she thought; and suddenly, irrationally, had the urge to kiss those satiny cheeks, to bury her nose in his silky hair and breathe in his strangely sweet baby smell.

He's only on the bed with me because it's so chilly, she told herself; otherwise he'd be sleeping in my emptied-out steamer trunk. She pulled a pillow behind her, wedging it tight against her back so that she could lie propped on her side; she didn't want to roll on him if she dozed off. She listened to his soft breathing, anxiously waiting from breath to breath for him to wake. But he slept on, peacefully enclosed in the safe circle of her arms. And after a while, Miss Vandermeyer slept as well.

Writers

Andrew Caink was born in King's Lynn and now lives in London. His stories have appeared in 'Succour' and the anthology 'Talking to Strangers' (Intellect Books).

Nel Boswood has lived and worked in Devon for the past 11 years, where she is lucky enough to be surrounded by family and friends. In 2007 she began writing short stories, something she had been meaning to do for a long time and would now like to continue.

Seán Burke is the author of 'The Death and Return of the Author' (1992/8), 'Authorship' (1995), 'Deadwater' (2002), trans. 'Au bout des docks' (Rivages, 2007), 'The Ethics of Writing' (in press, Jan 2008). The research and early drafts for 'The Night of Nights' were made possible by an Academi Cymraig Writers' Bursary in 2005 for which Seán remains very grateful.

Jane Feaver was born in Durham. She is editor, with Michael Morpurgo, of 'Cock Crow', an anthology of poems about the countryside. Her first novel, 'According to Ruth', was published in 2007 by Harvill Secker. She works in Devon for the charity, Farms for City Children, and is studying for a PhD in Creative Writing at Exeter University.

David Gaffney lives in Manchester. His collections of ultra-short stories, 'Sawn Off Tales' (2006 Salt publishing) and 'Aromabingo' (2007 Salt Publishing) are both available now and his novel, 'Never Never', a tale of debt counselling and trepanning, is out in 2008 on Tindall Street Press.

Tania Hershman (www.taniahershman.com) is a former science journalist living in Jerusalem, a founder member of the Fiction Workhouse online writing collective and edits 'The Short Review'. Her short and very short stories have been published in a range of journals and anthologies and broadcast on BBC Radio 4. Her first collection, 'The White Road and Other Stories', will be published by Salt in 2008.

Luke Kennard achieved brief notoriety when he was shortlisted for the Forward Prize for Best Collection of Poetry 2007 for his second book 'The Harbour Beyond the Movie', available from Salt Publishing. His poetry and criticism have appeared in 'Stride Magazine', 'The Guardian' and the 'TLS'.

Eleanor Knight is a PhD student at Exeter University. She is writing a novel set in London's Victoria.

Lauri Kubuitsile is a writer living in Botswana. Her short stories have appeared in 'New Contrasts' (South Africa), 'Mslexia' (UK), 'Spinetingler' (USA) and 'Horizon Magazine' (Canada), among others. She has won numerous writing prizes; most recently first place in the 13th BTA/AngloPlatinum Short Story Contest.

Michael Morpurgo is the author of over one hundred books, and the winner of many literary prizes. Michael lives in Devon where he and his wife established the charity 'Farms for City Children' in 1976. He was awarded an OBE in 2006 for services to literature.

Sarah Oswald writes fiction inspired by places. She grew up in Canada, lived as a traveller, spent many years in Wales and now lives in Devon. It's her ambition to write something as beautiful and disturbing as walking on Dartmoor in the rain with no map and a podful of ISIS. Her story 'Roger's Emporium, Ad valorum' is due to appear in issue 31 of the 'White Wall Review' (Canada) in 2008.

Jean Rafferty is an award-winning journalist, most recently in the Norwich Union Medical Journalism Awards for an article on feeding the elderly in hospital. She is also the author of two books on sport, but is intent on moving into fiction and is writing a novel for the PhD programme at Strathclyde University.

Emma Seaman has a degree in English from Worcester College, Oxford, has followed a career in Marketing and has been writing for four years. Her short stories have been nominated for several awards and published in magazines and anthologies including 'Seven Days' and 'The Remarkable Everyday' (from www.legendpress.co.uk).

Robin Sidwell lives in Birmingham and holds an MA in Writing from the University of Warwick and a BA in Creative studies from Bath Spa University. His short stories have been short listed for the Derek Walcott Prize and the Fish Knife Award. He is currently working on a novel and hopes to find an agent when it is completed.

Martin Sorrell has published several translations of French plays and of French and Spanish poetry, and has written plays and stories for Radio 4. Two of his translations have won BCLA/John Dryden prizes, and one original play a Mental Health Media Award for Best Radio Drama.